Lily

I0562649

Dorothy W. Cosey

Lily

ISBN:
ISBN 978-1-105-10339-1
90000

9 781105 103391

DEDICATION

I dedicate this book to my family, and my four loving daughter's, Andrea, NaQuisha, Ashley, Keri, and last but not least my son Willie Maurice Jr.

I also dedicate this book to my former husband for supporting me, and encouraging me to continue with my dreams. Thank, you Maurice. It takes a lot of understanding, and forgiveness having late dinners. I love you all.

Lily

CONTENTS

Lily

ACKNOWLEDGMENTS

I would like to thank all my fans who love adventure and mystery in each romance novel they read. I would like to thank God for blessing me each day, and for his great mercy.

Lily

Prologue:

In 1898, the United States was in the process of healing after the civil war. Small numbers of African Americans were coming into their own, some discovered ways to make an income and survive. The Thomas family was one of the fortunate families to succeed at being cattle ranchers.

Lily's father earned his freedom fighting in the civil war, and worked the land as a farmer. His one pride in this world was his daughter Lily. Even though life was not always fair growing up with a mixed heritage, she endures the teasing, and the jealousy. After Lily meets Bradley Thomas, the door of privilege open up for her, and life takes a dramatic turn. Follow one woman's sacrifice and sorrow to be with the man she loves.

Dorothy W. Cosey

Chapter One

Lily was born on a farm west of Tennessee, and struggles with prejudice, love, sorrow, and survival.

Thomas and Margarita Kendal's life consist of simple pleasures. They were poor folk who know the value of a dollar, both born of Indian and Negro descent. Thomas features consist of high cheekbones, wavy jet-black hair, and grey eyes. Margarita is a tall slim woman with flowing jet-black hair, and caramel skin.

The Kendal family are proud of their roots, and work long tiring hours in their fields. Thomas walks toward his wife with a comforting smile on his face. He was amazed, it takes many years making ends meet, and to purchase a home with land.

Thomas takes comfort with his life at least he was a free man unlike his Grandfather. He earned his freedom after serving in the Military. Thomas finds a seat and replies. "Come over here and relax you can't stay out in the fields any more darling we have this child to be concerned with now."

Margarita's face breaks into a warm and loving smile. "You are right Thomas. I feel as if I will pop they both laugh at the remark. Thomas was looking forward to his first child.

He prayed for a son, if not he would love a daughter as much as Margarita. On June 1880, a daughter named Lily was born. Thomas reflects on his time with his wife and daughter. The years passed quicker than he remembers, and he questions were the time went. Lily was a full-grown woman at eighteen years old, and it makes Thomas feel like an old man.

Thomas and Lily sit along the riverbank each Sunday after church. Sunday is the only day available for Thomas to spend with his only child. Most days Thomas spends in his fields working. He looks at his daughter with pride, she has

blossom into a beautiful young woman. Lily
has his grey eyes, curly long hair and
smooth brown skin. Thomas admits suitors
would soon come to call on Lily. He
questions if he was ready to let go of his
baby.

He breathes a sigh, accepting the fact
that he has no choice in the matter. One day
she would have a family of her own. "You
know how much your mother and I love you
Lily." Thomas replies. Lily turns to face her
father, her grey eyes sparkle with love, and
admiration. "Of course I do father! Is
something wrong?"

The expression on her face displays
worry, Thomas quickly dispels her fears.
"No! Lily, I just want you to know that." It
was getting late, time to head for home.
They gather the fish and their handmade
fishing poles, and start in the direction
home.

Margarita was making the side
dishes for their meal one thing she could
count on was Thomas and Lily bringing
home a nice catch. It was not long before

Lily and Thomas enter the backdoor. "You two keep me very busy". Margarita exclaims. Lily enters the kitchen with Thomas in tow she offers to help her mother clean and prepare dinner.

Lily was placing the dishes on the table while Margarita was preparing the food. Once she completes the task setting the table. She helps her mother serve the meal. As soon as the family sits down at the dinner table, there was a loud knock at the door.

Thomas is curious not many visitors stop by at this time of day. He places his napkin on the table and goes to answer the door. Thomas was not expecting the man standing at the doorstep. The man is a tall, brown-skin man, with light brown eyes, and wavy hair.

He was well dressed, and judging from his appearance, he is some type of businessperson. "Good day, May I help you sir?" Thomas replies.

Lily

The stranger smiles at Thomas displaying straight white teeth. He answers the question in a baritone voice, and Thomas could tell the man has a good education by his speech. There was no way this man could possibly be from around these parts.

"Hello, my name is Bradley Thomas. I have been travelling for some hours, and wonder if I may trouble you for a night of shelter. I 'am willing to pay you for your trouble."

Thomas assumption is correct the man standing in his doorway was no common thief. He assumes the man is lost or just exhausted from his journey, and decides to offer his assistance. "I will not take your money sir. I can provide you with shelter.

Come in, out the cold, and let me introduce you to my family. Bradley instantly likes this man. Thomas was honest, straight forward, and hardworking judging from his home indicates his assumption is correct.

Bradley silently observes Thomas accessing his character. His conclusion is Thomas was plain friendly and honest. The way Thomas carries himself is one indication that he is a proud man. He continues to the dining room "Please join us for dinner." Thomas replies.

Bradley walks deeper into the room and removes his hat, and coat. He thanks Thomas for inviting him to his table. "That is most kind of you. May I call you Thomas?" Bradley asks.

Thomas grins at Bradley; no one has ever asked that question. His eyes twinkle with amusement. "Sir, as long as I may call you by your given name, Thomas is fine."

Thomas extends his hand to Bradley and the men hit it off instantly both respecting the other. Thomas makes the introductions starting with his wife. Margarita gives Bradley a welcoming smile and replies. " It is very nice to meet you."

Thomas introduces Bradley to Lily, and Bradley draws a deep breath, not expecting such a beautiful woman. She is average height with curly long hair, and eyes the color of liquid silver. Bradley finds her very attractive and a distraction.

She was a very striking woman but unaware of her beauty. "Hello, Lily it is very nice to meet you." Lily was use to the town's men in her area, and most are farmers, not like this man. He is well dressed as if attending church, and sophisticated.

Actually, he was the best-looking man she has ever met. They sit down at the dinner table Thomas and Bradley are talking as if they have known each other all their lives.

Bradley was a good conversationalist, and he compliments Margarita. "You have a lovely home." She is delighted that Bradley appreciates her hard work maintaining their home.

He turns his attention to Lily, and begins to ask questions, but Lily was deep in thought about the stranger at her table. She was so preoccupied with the man that she ignores Bradley's question. She was too busy absorbing every detail about him.

The way his eyebrows arch when he was amused, and the long lashes that surround light brown eyes. Bradley attempts to repeat the question.

She abruptly snaps out of her reverie, and turns her attention back to Bradley. Chagrin shadows her features, while he was dissecting her with his eyes. His stare is so intense; it feels like he is reading her mind. "Oh, I 'am sorry Bradley. You were saying." Bradley raises one brow at Lily.

He has a good idea that she is daydreaming. A smile touches his lips and he winks at her. Lily became even more uncomfortable, chiding herself for looking like a complete fool.

She lifts her head and listens to the question once again. "I was asking you if you have a steady beau." Lily was not expecting the question, and her eyes go wide with surprise. His bold remark catches her off guard.

When she answers the question, her voice stumbles over each word. "Oh no, no, I do not have a beau." Bradley continues conversation, but not once did he release her from his gaze. After he was satisfied his gaze shifts to her parents.

His next remark leaves her breathless. "The men in your area must be absolutely blind." It takes Lily a couple of minutes to respond. His blunt statement shocks her, not use to anyone so outspoken. "I guess." Lily answers in a nervous tone.

She was fascinating to Bradley, and his mind was working overtime. He was determined to get to know her better. A plan was forming, but the first step is to ask for permission from her father.

He turns his attention back to her parents. Thomas noticed Bradley's preoccupation with Lily, and he asks Bradley to join him out on the porch. Thomas was not a fool, it was obvious

Bradley is smitten with Lily, and Thomas being a protective father, has some questions of his own.

Lily and Margarita clear the dishes from the dinner table. Margarita was aware that Lily is very impressed with Bradley. There was no comparison between Bradley and the young men Lily was accustom too. He was different well educated, handsome, and experienced.

Margarita begins the conversation. "What do you think of Bradley?" Margarita waits for her daughters reply. "He is very eloquent mother, and handsome to boot." Margarita warns her daughter. "Take care Lily he is a man of experience, and I don't want your heart broken."

Lily appreciates her mother's candour. She grins. "Don't worry mother he surely has a wife waiting for him." "You never know dear just be careful." Lily decides to let the conversation drop, after all, she just met this man, what did she know about him anyway?

Lily

Lily chides herself, stop thinking about those light brown eyes, his beautiful smile, and get a grip, Lily. Thomas and Bradley are discussing his position, and marital status.

Bradley explains to Thomas that he is a rancher, and the overseer of his father's business. There is no misses Thomas, and would love to have a wife, if she was the right woman.

Bradley shares with Thomas that he would like to court his daughter. He waits for Thomas to reply. Thomas stands looking Bradley straight in the eye. "Lily is my only child. I want what is best for her. Bradley, if you have honorable intentions regarding Lily. You have my blessing."

Thomas informs Bradley the rest was up to Lily. Bradley made the decision that very day. He wants Lily and he was destined to have her. He contemplates how to proceed with his courting of Lily. Every part of him desires her, and he is certain she would make an excellent wife. Thomas and Margarita excuse themselves to their rooms.

Bradley takes this opportunity to be better acquainted. He asks Lily to join him on the porch, and he sits with her on the porch swing. The closeness was nerve wrecking and she embraces the scent of his cologne, and male vigour.

He begins the conversation with stories of a rancher's life, and she listens in awe. His presence overwhelms her, not to mention his strength, and courage.

Bradley shares with Lily his desire to have a wife and family. She listens intently, and falls deeper under his spell. Was it possible to fall for someone in a first meeting? Was she losing her mind? These thoughts plague her conscience. None of that matters because Lily was already lost after meeting Bradley.

The moon was full tonight and combination of being in close proximity with Bradley on the porch swing intensifies the effect on Lily. The attraction engulfs her as a moth to the flame.

Lily

She feels his strong hands touching her shoulders. Bradley draws her closer against him, and lowers his mouth to her lips. His tongue is warm and sensual probing deeper. The first time Bradley kisses Lily he instantly wants more.

He dips his tongue deeper into her depths, and closes the distance between them on the swing. She accepts his embrace, and Bradley releases a moan of pleasure. Kissing her was like fire in his soul.

He has to put distance between them because his loins are burning with desire. Bradley uses restraint not wanting to self-indulge with his desire. The last thing he wants is to frighten her away.

It was obvious from her unschooled kisses that she is still a virgin, and he would not take advantage of her innocence. She would remain a virgin until they are married.

Lily was experiencing a hunger she could not explain. At this moment all she knows is she wants more. Her emotions are out of control, she was unable to comprehend this new longing deep inside.

This was something new to her, and she continues to cling to Bradley. Until she realizes he has put distance between them.

"What is wrong?" Lily asks, with eyes wide open. "Darling, I have to release you. You have a strange effect on me." A moan of frustration escapes him, and he bows his head to kiss Lily again. He was playing with fire and knows it. This time he puts his arms out, to keep Lily at bay.

She witness first-hand the affect she was having on Bradley. Maybe she has better stop. Lily was not experienced, and she has no clue how to share intimacy with a man. Bradley rises from the swing and pulls Lily into his arms. He uses better judgment, and walks with her to the door. "Goodnight Lily sweet dreams." He places a kiss on her forehead.

He was turning to leave, and she wants more, but she enters her room with Bradley on her mind the whole time. The night was miserable for Bradley. He tosses and turns most of the night. What was wrong with him? This woman ignites passion and lust in him something that was hard for him to comprehend. Bradley has had his share of women before, but none of them could captivate him like her.

He has to admit, Lily is the one, and he decides to ask for her hand in marriage first thing in the morning. Morning arrives Bradley was up early that morning. He shaves, and cleans up for the day. Thomas was up and having a cup of coffee, and asks Bradley to join him.

The two men sit down over coffee, and discuss his proposal. It takes courage to ask for permission to marry Lily. Thomas thinks on the matter before he agrees. Bradley was a good man for his daughter of that he was sure. He could offer Lily a life of comfort. Thomas was not a wealthy man, and he wants more for his daughter. They decide to discuss the marriage with the women.

Lily wakes with the new day, and thinks of nothing except Bradley. Remembering his kiss sends chills down her spine. She could still feel his strong hands caressing her flesh. She admits he is the man for her. Each time she thinks of him her pulse quickens.

Meeting him was a blessing, and a pleasure. The family sits down over breakfast to discuss the proposal, and Lily's hand in marriage. Margarita was agreeable Lily was ecstatic. Bradley, make his proposal on one knee with Lily's hand in his, looking into her grey eyes.

"Lily, I know this is sudden. In my heart, I know you are the one for me. Will you do me the honor of marriage? I cannot live without you." A warm feeling overtakes Lily. She prayed so hard to find someone to love, and God answers her prayers. Standing before her was Bradley the man she loves. Tears of joy slide down her cheeks. "Yes, Bradley." Her voice cracks. "It would be my pleasure to be your wife."

At first, he was holding his breath, and then he stands quickly. Bradley picks Lily up by the waist, and hugs her to him. He swings her around. "I will make you happy Lily! We will have a good life together." Margarita interrupts the couple for one brief moment.

"Bradley, how much time before the wedding will take place?" He places Lily on her feet and answers. "It should be no more than a couple of weeks. My family would want to attend." Margarita replies. "Then Lily that means we need to get you fitted for a grown as soon as possible." Bradley offers monetary support for their wedding.

Thomas respects Bradley, if he had any doubts about him they went out the window. Thomas was positive his decision was the right one. After breakfast, Margarita and Lily inform the men they are going into town. They need to purchase material, and have Lily fitted for her gown.

Bradley agrees. He has business to conduct in town. After many hours of fittings, they leave for home. Bradley rides in silence with Thomas. He was reading a telegram from his brother with distressing news. Bradley decides to discuss the matter with Lily in private.

Chapter Two

Thomas calls, to Margarita, after briefly speaking with Bradley. After Thomas and Margarita leave, Bradley searches for Lily.

He finds her in the hallway. "Lily will you join me for a walk?" She answers his question without hesitation. "I would love to."

Long strides take Bradley across the hallway. This yearning feeling was new to him; it left him feeling complete. Lily is a piece of the puzzle that he has been missing in his life. She completes him.

He places his arm around Lily's waist and guides her out the door. Tonight was another full moon, and Bradley takes this opportunity to speak with Lily. He steps toward Lily with a strange look on his face. "What is it? Is something wrong?' Lily asks."

"I have received news that my mother has taken ill. I must return to St. Louis in the morning." I have discussed the situation with your father. Lily we need to get married in the morning. You will return with me to St. Louis. ---" He pauses for one moment before continuing. "Sweet heart, I know, this is not the wedding you wished for, but under the circumstances I have no choice."

Bradley has a frown on his handsome face. Lily digests the information then responds. "For one moment I was afraid that you changed your mind about the wedding. My place is with you now. If we need to leave right away, I accept that."

Bradley draws, Lily closer in his arms. In a tone barely audible, he replies. "Choosing you for my wife was the best decision I have ever made. You have my promise darling. I will make this up to you." Lily lifts her head from his shoulder.

He could see the sincerity in her eyes, "I am so happy Bradley." It touches him deep. Lily was young with no worldly experience, but she loves him unconditionally. He bows his head to claim her sweet lips. Bradley kissed his future wife deeply, and without inhibition. It was a long, passionate kiss. When he releases her, she is breathing erratically. Bradley slowly lifts his head, and notices the passion in her eyes.

It was hard to resist her, after he manages to get his emotions under control he replies. "You will meet my entire family." A nervousness creeps over her. "How many, are in your family?"

Bradley grins, and then replies. "Well, I have two brothers, Aaron, and Daniel, and my sisters Thelma, and Monica, my parent's, Helen, and William."

Reality hits Lily. She knows very little about Bradley and she questions if his family would approve of her. What will she do if they do not like her? Insecurity was getting the best of her.

"Bradley senses apprehension. The expression on her face looks strained.

"Don't worry darling, my family will love you, as much as I do." Her tensions ease, and Bradley feels her body relax in his arms.

Lily exhales her breath as his words comfort her. Bradley was becoming an important part of her life. He places his arm around her small waist. They walk side by side to discuss the change of plans with her parents.

Thomas and Margarita are in the living room. Bradley and Lily join the couple and Bradley takes the opportunity to discuss the change of plans. He clears his throat, and begins the conversation.

"Thomas there has been an unexpected turn of events. It puts Lily and me in an awkward position. My mother has taken ill, and I must return on the morning train. We have to get married sooner than planned. I will not leave without Lily by my side."

Thomas thinks on the matter what other options are there. His daughter would be unforgiving if he objects. Her happiness was his main priority. He rubs his chin before he replies. "I was not prepared for this news Bradley.

We want Lily to have a wedding to remember, but under these circumstances, you must be with your family. We understand."

Margarita listens to the exchange between her husband, and Bradley. She replies. "We will miss you Lily. I wish we could give you a fancy wedding." Lily touches Margarita's hand.

"I will miss you both, we can always visit, and Mother a large wedding doesn't matter to me. I love you." Margarita hugs Lily, and her future son-in law. Thomas formally welcomes Bradley into the family. The two men are friends, and Thomas would not have entrusted his daughter with anyone else.

He is certain Bradley would take excellent care of his daughter. The women leave to prepare dinner. Thomas and

Bradley are still in deep conversation.
Margarita replies.

"Look, at those two. You would
think they have known each other all their
lives." Lily peeks around the corner at the
two men, and her heart fills with joy. She
was glad Thomas likes her future husband.
Margarita admits Bradley was a good catch
for Lily. The women serve dinner. Bradley
comments, on the fried chicken, "Mother
Kendal this chicken is delicious.

The whole meal is outstanding."
"Thank you, Bradley. Lily is a very good
cook also." Bradley was surprised. He looks
in Lily's direction, with a devilish smile, and
winks. She demurely lowers her lashes a bit
shy.

Margarita was asking Bradley about
St. Louis. "So Bradley, when will we see
the two of you after you are married?"
Bradley was sharp and very attentive to
Margarita's question. "I hope that we will
return here in about six months.

Lily

I 'am considering building a home here in Tennessee. That is if Lily approves." Bradley turns his attention to his future wife. Lily was very surprised. "I could ask for nothing better Bradley."

Lily knew Bradley was making this decision to keep her close to her parents. She smiles at Bradley and whispers. "Thank you so much love." Bradley smiles in return. He took in consideration Lily's youth, she still needs the closeness of her family, and it was the right thing to do. It would keep Lily happy to be with the two main people in her life.

After dinner, Bradley and Thomas retire to the living room for brandy and coffee. The two men had much to discuss. Lily and her mother finish the dishes. Margarita replies. "I had better make it an early night.

The priest will be here in the morning." Lily kisses her mother on the cheek, and bids her good night. She was walking towards her room. Bradley was finish talking with Thomas, and asks Lily to go for a walk with him. Her nostrils embrace the fragrance of water and flowers at full bloom. "I have never known such contentment in my whole life."

Bradley enfolds Lily into his arms he stares deep into her eyes as if he was searching her very soul. His hands gently massage her smooth shoulders, as his tongue traces a path from her neck to the outline of her breast.

Her breath catches in her throat, as his hands roamed over her full figure. His breathing increases and he lowers his hands touching the mounds of her backside. Their bodies became one as he draws her closer. Lily feels his manhood at full peak against her thigh.

A tide of emotion overflows once more, and a soft moan escapes her lips. Her mouth opens like a flower waiting on the rain welcoming his kiss. Their tongues dance together in an erotic motion stirring a forceful passion that leaves them both hungry for more.

Lily

A moan escapes Bradley, as he places light kisses over Lily's neck. She never imagined passion could be like this, it made her want to experience the pleasure shared between a man and woman.

He was lost in a vortex of desire, and it was a new emotion astounds him. Bradley was always the one to ignite passion in women, but Lily was not like other woman she was different. No other woman made him experience all the love he feels for her.

He was losing his will power, she made him want to make love to her right on the spot, but his better judgment takes hold and he regrets having to end the kiss.

Her breathing was erratic, and her eyes are bright with passion. Lily wants more! She looks up at Bradley with a questioning stare. "Please don't stop, not now."

"I have to love; until we wed then I will make you mine." He hugs Lily close to his heart, while trying to slow his breathing.

They continue their walk in silence each longing to finish what started as a simple kiss. Bradley finds it hard to focus she was a welcome distraction. Lily was unsure how much longer she could hold out, each time she is in his arms she forgets all reason.

Bradley walks, Lily back to the house, she was reaching for the doorknob then stops. She was having a hard time adjusting to the new feelings of need. He tries to ease the tension by hugging her close, and placing a kiss on her forehead.

His voice was barley a whisper. "Goodnight Lily, sleep well." He releases his hold and turns to leave. Lily enters her room with mixed emotions. A part of her wants to make love to Bradley, and she was ashamed of her wanton actions.

Bradley apparently loves the way she responds to his lovemaking. The only problem was she had nothing to compare it too. When she finally falls to sleep dreams of long nights filled with shared passion torments her.

Lily

Bradley enters his room with a grimace on his face. Right across the hall was a woman that he could spend an eternity loving. She was passionate, sensual, and loving. He lies in bed uncomfortable, and body rebelling with need.

It was damn hard to refuse Lily. She was so beautiful and innocent. There was a vixen inside of her waiting to be set free. Only he would explore the desire that sleeps within her. It was getting more difficult to contain his desire around her, and he tries to push the memory of her out of his mind by thinking about tomorrow.

Lily will be my wife to love in every way and that very thought put a smile on his face. The next morning was chaotic with preparations. The priest arrives on time, and Margarita scrambles to fix Lily's hair. Bradley pays the dressmaker extra to have Lily's dress ready by morning.

Thomas escorts his daughter down the aisle. Bradley places a wedding band on Lily's finger and the two unite as man and wife. Bradley shakes Thomas hand and hugs

Margarita. "You have my word. I will bring your daughter home to visit you both." Bradley replies.

This was an emotional time for Lily she has never ventured away from home. She rushes into her parent's embrace with tears glisten her eyes. "I love you two and I shall miss you terribly."

It was time to go to the train station, and Thomas and Margarita join the couple. Bradley informs Thomas that one of his men would collect his horse. Once at the train station, she hugs her folks once again dabbing at her eyes. Bradley helps Lily board the train. The next thing she remembers is sharing a seat with her husband.

It gives her a chance to admire the man next to her. The problem is she is not the only one admiring her husband. Several women could not keep their eyes off him. Lily feels proud he was all hers, and she was not one to share the love of her life.

Lily

Bradley interrupts her thoughts. "Darling, I hope you enjoy the trip to my parent's. I just wish it was under happier circumstances." She tries to sound confident. "Bradley my love, we can get though any thing together." She covers his hand with hers giving him the strength to face the unknown.

He welcomes her strength, and support. She was his rock and all her needs. The ride was long it takes about three day's to arrive in St. Louis. When the couple exits, the train a handsome man was waiting for Bradley and Lily and he greets them both.

The man waiting is tall, graceful, and gives Lily an approving eye. He introduces himself as Aaron, and she knows right away that he is Bradley's brother. Aaron helps with their luggage. The two men hug one another then Bradley formally introduces Lily to Aaron as his wife.

"You have excellent taste brother, hello Lily. Please do not believe anything Brad tells you." Lily chuckles with laughter. She likes Aaron he has a very good sense of humour.

Bradley was questioning Aaron about their mother Helen. "How is mother doing?"

Aaron replies. "You will have to see mother for yourself, then you decide what you think we should do." Aaron is the eldest son. "How is father holding up?" Bradley asks. "Right now he is doing as best as he can, you know William! He's tough."

The two brothers laugh. Lily admires the closeness between the two. She sits back in her seat and enjoys the beautiful scenery. They were pulling up to a grand white house with a large veranda. The house is circular with flowers, and wide stone steps.

The driveway is cobbled. The only time she saw homes like this is in passing and rich families owned them.

Bradley announces they are at their destination. He notices the surprise on Lily's face. She looks like a scared rabbit ready to take flight, and he feels her fear. "Don't worry sweetheart my family will love you as I do." Bradley's words were comforting.

She feels out of place. There was a short woman with a man in uniform waiting for them to exit the buggy. The man was the butler and the woman the house cleaner. Bradley helps Lily down from the buggy. The tall butler speaks first. "Good day, Mr Thomas."

The woman is rude she greets Bradley and ignores Lily. "Hello sir." Bradley puts his arm around his wife's waist and walks toward the house. Aaron follows close behind they enter the foyer, and Lily scans her surroundings.

The house furnished lavishly with crystal chandeliers, expensive furniture, and large mahogany staircase. The floors have expensive throw rugs on hard wood. It did not take Lily long to realise this home belongs to people of wealth.

She stops in her tracks to ask her husband a question. "You are willing to give this up for me?" Bradley pauses, and looks down into his wife's shocked face before answering her question. "This means nothing to me Lily."

She could not even imagine giving up this sort of life, nor could she imagine ever being without Bradley. She places her hand in his, craning her neck to look at him directly. "This doesn't matter to me, I love you. You know that don't you?"

Bradley could see the sincerity in her face, and he knew she spoke the truth. "Come on darling, we have to see my mother." Aaron interrupts for one second. He mentions to the couple not to worry he would alert the family of Brad's arrival and his new wife.

Bradley guides his wife up the large staircase, and she notices the entire wall covered in beautiful African and Indian artwork. The long steps have thick plush carpet. Bradley and Lily walk together down the long hallway.

Lily

She counts at least six bedrooms on this floor alone. They walk further down the hall to the last room on the left. It was his parent's room.

Helen Thomas was sitting at her dressing table with a hairbrush in her hand. She glances at the mirror and catch the reflection of her son coming over to her.

A smile forms on her lips. "Here is my son. I knew nothing would keep you from me." Bradley walks closer toward his mother. He leans over to kiss her on the forehead. "Hello mother, I want you to meet my wife Lily." Her eyes shift from Bradley to Lily.

Helen gives her the once over, and a smile touches her lips. "Come over here child. I won't bite you." Lily steps forward. "Hello." Lily replies, in a nervous voice. "It is nice to meet you." Good heavens Helen was about to make this child faint from worry.

She tries to break the ice. "My son has excellent taste in women. I hope that you and I can become great friends." "I would like that." Lily answers. Bradley is glad his mother approves of his choice, but he was not going to beat around the bush. He wants answers and poses his next question.

"Mother how you are feeling"? Her smile widens. "I feel much better now that you are here." William was entering the room. "Ah, Bradley you have arrived safely, and who is this lovely creature?"

Bradley makes the introductions. "Hello father this is my wife Lily, she is a God send to me." William walks toward Lily and extends a hand offering a warm welcome. "My dear it is a pleasure to meet you. I hope that you can keep my son in his place." William was smiling, and winks at Lily. "I will certainly try". She returns the smile.

His expression becomes serious when he speaks to Bradley. He stands to his full height and mentions the rest of the family is in the sitting room waiting. "They all want to meet your lovely wife.

Lily

We know that you had a very long journey and you two probably want to rest for an hour or two before dinner, then you can introduce your wife to the family." Bradley was agreeable to the suggestion.

It was a long trip, and Lily looks a little tired. She was thankful her husband was considerate enough to notice her discomfort. "Fine we will see you in a couple of hours my wife needs to rest."

He hugs his father and mother before taking his leave. Bradley assures both parents they would catch up on everything later. He shows Lily to their room. The room was large and spacious, and the side tables hold hand painted vases with flowers.

The bed covers are back, and a nightgown was at the foot of the big mahogany bed. Bradley asks the help to draw a bath for Lily. "Why don't you freshen up love, take a nap. I will wake you in a couple of hours, and we can meet my family together.

"A bath sounds wonderful darling, and I could use a nap." She walks over to her husband grateful for his thoughtfulness; actually, he was the most considerate man she has ever known. She places a kiss on his lips, and he returns the gesture by lightly brushing his mouth with hers, but it was distant.

He was trying to restrain himself with her. Bradley was not going to let this get out of hand. Her first time should be special, and he plans to teach her the art of making love. Tonight would be one that Lily would remember for the rest of her life. He would be her one, and only lover.

Bradley feels his manhood straining against the material, and eases her away from him before he explodes with desire. Gently he nudges her toward the bath.

Once Lily realizes he is not going to take it farther, she picks up the grown and starts for the bath. As she peels away, the dusty clothing from her body she glances at the large tub the water looks inviting.

Lily

She grabs the large plush towel, and wraps it around her body. Bradley was standing in the doorway watching her. The temptation was too great; he could not take it any longer being an observer. Watching her unclothed body drives him insane with need. He quickly removes his clothing to join his wife.

Chapter 3

Bradley places his hands around her waist drawing her closer. The contact with her naked flesh excites him beyond the imagination. She could feel the passion rising inside of him. He leans down to capture her lips, as a she releases a moan of pleasure.

All of his reserve stripped away, she tastes so good. He was in a world of sensation, touching her in the most intimate places. Lily let go of all her fears something was driving her on, she was touching his body not sure what to do but following her instincts.

She caresses his long lengthy body, enjoying the throatily sounds coming from him. She lets her hand drift lower around his manhood. He shudders from her touch, and deepens the kiss stroking her mouth with his tongue, placing his hands between her thighs stroking her into a state of ecstasy.

Lily

His mouth moves from her lips to her breast, massaging each one, kneading them like dough. She feels his warm mouth on the tips suckling them until they became erect. She was going out of her mind, if making love feels like this then it was wonderful.

His hands continue searching her completely he holds on to her guiding her back to the tub. She follows his lead. Once he enters the tub, and positions her on top of him. He removes the soap from the dish and lathers his hands.

He covers every inch of her body with the soap, and massages places she never thought exist. Something was happening her body begins to shake out of control. There was no pain just an indescribable emotion making her body tingle all over.

It was her first climax. A voice that sounds foreign to her ears is mumbling incoherently. "Oh my God Bradley, what are you doing to me? Please don't stop, I want it." Her sounds of passion push him over the edge. He moves her forward and exits the tub. She clings to his outstretched hand, as he helps her out the tub.

He lifts her in his arms and carries her to the bed. Once she is settled, he lies beside her, drawing her closer to resume the loving. Need makes his body tremble from excitement and anticipation. His mouth seeks hers, and the fire ignites once more, as his tongue finds the nectar within. Lily returns his passion, and swirls her tongue within his mouth. This was a new lesson and she enjoyed it.

She hears his moans of pleasure as his hands strokes her body. She moves her head from side to side, but jerks in surprise when his fingers enter her core. Hot creamy moisture surrounds her core, and his fingers dip in and out moving in rhythm.

Her hips are moving with the motion of his hand pushing in every direction. Oh, no she was having one of those feelings again. Her body is responding to everything he does.

Moans of pleasure overtake Lily, and she is incoherent, calling Bradley's name aloud. "Bradley, I love you. Darling, please make me feel this way forever." He whispers in a hoarse voice. "I promise Lily to make you feel like this every night."

A tremor of excitement rushes through his loins. Lily crested on a tide of ecstasy lost in pure sensation. Bradley was ready to take it farther he slides his body lower tasting the sweet nectar of her, as his hands caress inner thighs, until she begs for release.

Lily is not sure of what she was asking for, but needs completion. Bradley continues loving her lower half, moving upward to kiss her again, this time he spreads her legs to receive him. She is still riding wave after wave of ecstasy. Her body is sensitive tingling from ecstasy and she does not notice Bradley positioning her for completion.

Once he was satisfied. He continues lifting her higher in the climax. She feels his warm arousal touching her pushing its way in, and sharp pain sears her body. She is about to scream from the piercing pain.

Bradley coaxes her on, being as gentle with her as possible, he places kisses on her cheeks while moving his hips up and down. She follows his lead. When he enters her tight core, Lily was moving with him in unison. She clings to his wide shoulders still incoherent.

"Love me Bradley, just love me." She breathes. He answers her plea. "I will love you Lily just relax and give yourself to me." She obeys his request, relaxing her body to allow him entrance once he fills the tight space, the pain stops.

She feels a rush of pleasure, and this time, she was so high, she could swear, she left her body. Bradley holds her tight making her melt inside him they became one. He is ready for release pumping his hips quickly he lets out a roar and empties himself inside her.

Lily

After the love, making the two lay there exhausted, before sleep arrives. When Lily wakes, she is alone. She spends a few minutes thinking about the passionate love she just made to Bradley. A smile touches her lips. She stretches her body, feeling a little sore, then rolls out of the bed scrambling to her feet, wondering if she has overslept.

She hurries into the bathroom to freshen up briskly brushing her long hair. Lily exits the room and walks down the long empty hallway. As she makes her way down the steps sounds of angry voices echo, and they were getting louder.

When she reaches the bottom of the stairs, she recognizes that deep smooth voice. It was Bradley and he sounds impatient. The other voice was a woman. Lily did not know who she was. She could hear the woman talking to Bradley.

"What the hell is this Bradley? Who is the half-bred tramp that you have married? Wasn't I woman enough for you?" This conversation was getting on his nerves.

Elaine was making him lose patience, his eyes were dark from anger and he glares at her. "I will not have you speaking ill about my wife.

Her name is Lily, and the rest is none of your damned business." The woman was clearly hysterical. "How could you do this to me Bradley? You know how much I love you. If you were going to marry any one it should have been me not that whore. I am the woman that you are in love with."

Bradley was furious. "Enough! Elaine, I want you to leave! You and I have been over a long time ago." There was a loud crash, the sound of glass breaking. Lily thought her heart would fall out of her chest after overhearing the last parting words of the woman.

"Only I will be your wife, you can count on that. This is not over!" The door slams behind the woman, and she was gone. Lily was in shock and disbelief. Who was this Elaine, and what was she to Bradley? She was certainly going to find out.

Lily

After calming her nerves, she walks into the room. Bradley was staring out the window. He turns around when she enters the room.

Bradley notes the expression on her face, and strides over in her direction. "Hello love, did you sleep well?" Lily places a light kiss on his cheek. It was not the loving passionate woman he made love to earlier, something was amiss with Lily.

"Is everything alright love?" It was her turn to ask the questions. The insecurity was too much for her. This episode upsets her greatly only Bradley could answer her questions. Her voice is shaky when she replies. "Who, who, is Elaine? Please tell me the truth Bradley."

He glances at his wife for a brief moment his mind reeling from the previous episode. He exhales his breath before he answers. It did not take a scientist to realize she was upset and angry.

Judging from the look on her face, she overheard the confrontation between him and Elaine. Bradley lowers his raised eyebrow. He answers the question staring her straight in the eye. "She was a woman that I thought, I was in love with. I was going to eventually marry her but it just didn't work out."

She was holding her breathe afraid of his answer. She lowers her head and asks the next question. "Are you still in love with her?" Bradley put his hands on her shoulders turning her to face him.

"I'm in love with my wife! I loved her the very first day I saw her. I stopped in for a night of shelter, and there she was. That woman was you Lily and I have no regrets." She releases her breath, and puts her arms around his neck pulling his face close to kiss his lips.

"I love you Bradley. I was so afraid that you were still in love with her. I did not know what else to do." He pulls his wife into his arms reassuring her. "You don't have to worry Lily. I would never hurt you. Can we go now? My family is waiting to meet you."

She links her arm with his and they enter the dining room together. The seating arrangement is to her liking, and her place at the table is next to Bradley. The family was there waiting patiently for Bradley to make the introductions.

He starts the introductions. This is Daniel my youngest brother, Daniel was a replica of Bradley he was a bit shorter. He introduces his sisters Monica and Thelma. Lily likes Thelma she was petite with a friendly personality.

Monica, on the other hand is a beautiful woman, but her looks do not compensate for her lack of personality. She was arrogant; you could tell Monica gets what Monica wants. It was obvious to Lily that Monica does not like her at all.

Bradley concludes the introductions with Aaron and William. Helen was absent from the table she was not feeling well. The family was discussing their mother's condition. Aaron was the first one to broach the subject. "Bradley we have constant concerns about mother and her forgetfulness.

There are times when she wonders off or misplace things. Thelma comments. "I have read about a condition of the brain. There may possibly be a tumour, little is known about this, but it is said that it could cause forgetfulness." Thelma was studying to be a Doctor.

"I think we should call Doctor Burns to have a look at mother." Daniel comments. William listens to his children everyone is worried about Helen including him. William decides it was time to stop the guessing and find out for sure.

He shares this information with his family. "I plan on taking your mother to the Doctor personally. Something has to be done right now, are we all in agreement?"

Bradley listens to his father and siblings. He volunteers his thoughts on the matter. "Father I trust your judgment. I also think mother needs to see a professional, all I want is for her to be healthy again."

Once the family members all agree on the decision, Monica suggests the women retire to the parlour, while the men talk. Lily glances over at Bradley. He knows she is a little apprehensive, but he encourages her to join his sisters. "Lily, darling, will you please join my sisters? I need to talk with my father and brothers for a few minutes."

"Of course love as you wish." Lily was hoping for a life raft. She was dreading being in Monica's company. Instead, she hides her dismay from Bradley. He exits the table and walks with his wife and sisters to the parlour.

Lily and Bradley walk behind the others, and he uses the opportunity to talk with his wife. "Lily thanks for being so supportive." "I'm your wife Bradley, anytime you need me I will be here."

They are in front of the parlour door Lily kisses her husband lightly on the cheek. She squares her shoulder before entering the room with her in-laws. Once inside the room Lily feels trapped, experiencing a foreboding about this meeting.

Monica waits for the women to take a seat. She was curious about Lily, and Bradley was not around to protect her. She was going to take the gloves off now no more pretending.

Monica was sizing Lily up, what a charity case this marriage was a sham. Bradley could choose any wealthy woman he wants, but instead he settles for this little half- breed.

Monica did not care for Lily the moment she met her. It was time to start her interrogation of Lily. "Well, Lily what types of schools have you attend?" Lily was not expecting the question, she was a farmer's daughter not some highbred snob.

"I have not attended any public or private schools just home schooling." Monica wrinkles her nose at Lily as if she was some foul odor. "Really, you're telling

Lily

me you married my brother without any
formal education?

It is obvious you have no money,
and what really bothers me is you are a half-
breed?" Lily could not believe this was
happening her mouth goes dry and she is
speechless, no one has ever treated her cruel
like this before. She covers her face as the
tears begin to moisten her cheeks.

Thelma is shame of her sister's
actions. She sees how devastated Lily is and
she is instantly angry. "Monica there is no
cause for that. Lily, please forgive Monica
and her rudeness." Monica was only
beginning she was not finished with Lily
yet.

She could care less about Lily, and
her feelings. Monica does not like Lily at all,
and she enjoys watching Lily squirm. "I
don't' know why my brother selected you,
when he could have done so much better
than a low life half-bred vagrant like
yourself."

That was the final straw. Thelma once again interrupts Monica. "I will not stand here listening to you speak to Lily in this way, she has done nothing to you, leave her be!" Thelma has never challenged Monica, but today Monica sees the determination in Thelma's eyes.

Monica decides to let it go for now, but not without a parting shot. "You are a gold digger." Monica flounces out the room. Thelma goes over to Lily. She was in tears. "I 'am so, sorry, I apologize for my sisters rudeness, she can be a bitch sometimes.

Please pay Monica no mind." Thelma was trying to comfort Lily. Her grey eyes were cloudy. "Thelma I do love Bradley! I had no idea he was so well off. I truly love him with all my heart." She broke into another round of tears.

Thelma sits next to Lily and gives her a hug. She takes one look at the girl, and knows she is telling the truth. There was a knock on the door, and Bradley enters the room. His eyes narrow when he glances at his wife, and his sister. Something was

wrong why else would his wife be in tears.
His temper flares, looking at his distraught
wife. "Lily, what is wrong?" He walks over
to his wife.

Thelma explains to Bradley what
took place. He was furious. "I will deal with
Monica promptly." Bradley helps his wife to
her feet. "Darling please, calm down, I will
deal with Monica, come with me." This was
the first time Lily was insulted, and angry.
She brushes at her tears.

"No Bradley, this is something I
have to do. I can't have you fighting all my
battles." Bradley saw strength in Lily, he did
not notice before. "Are you sure, love I can
handle this for you." "No, Bradley! I will do
this myself".

He looks at Thelma then makes his
excuses for the night. Bradley explains to
Lily how much getting along with the family
means to him, but he was cross with
Monica, and her rudeness. After calming,
Lily down Bradley draws her close into his
arms, and whispers in her ear.

"Darling, no matter what Monica or anyone else has to say. Remember how much I love you." The words from Bradley were what she needs to hear. Lily molds her body against Bradley absorbing his strength, and instant passion surges between the two of them.

Bradley cups her full round breast in his strong hands, and suckles each one with loving care. Lily begins to tremble with pleasure, as his hands move to touch her womanly area, and his fingers gently stroke her.

She feels him massaging her, as he slides his fingers back and forth. Once again, Lily's body heats up as if she was on fire. She slides her hands over his backside feeling his strong buttocks. She moves lower caressing his thighs amazed at the hardness between his legs.

Bradley moans from her touch. She continues to explore him, and moves further down his body touching, feeling the stiffness of his organ. She was no longer shy with him. It came natural she wants to explore him fully. Bradley was holding his breath not believing how quickly his wife was learning how to satisfy him.

Damn he was having a hard time containing himself. He was ready to explode, but he holds on until he could not hold on any longer. She was driving him insane with need. He places her on the bed then joins her. Lily thought they would make love in the same position that was not the case.

This time Bradley is in a sitting position he instruct his wife to climb on top of him, and bend her knees into a swat position. She does as he says. His strong hands circle her waist and guide her over his manhood.

He pulls her closer into his chest and they rock back and forth, each time he takes her higher and higher until she experiences that wonderful feeling that astounds her once more.

Lily set his soul on fire with desire, this time he changes the position once more only this time he was on top and Lily beneath him, as he gently enters her. Lily was oblivious to anything else. They both lay together out of breathe. Lily speaks first. "I have never experienced so much passion in all my life love."

Bradley chuckles before replying. "There's more where that came from darling." The next morning Lily wakes to an empty bed. She figures Bradley was out running the ranch she lays there reminiscing about her wonderful husband and his sexual appetite.

The very thought brought a smile to Lily's face. Enough reminiscing she climbs out of bed, and takes a bath. The warm water help ease her stiff muscles. She steps out of the tub, goes over to the mirror picks up a comb, and fixes her long hair. When she is satisfied with the result, she dresses for breakfast. As she makes her way down stairs, she meets Thelma going in the same direction. "Good morning Lily." "Good morning Thelma."

Lily

The two women walk down the stairs together. Thelma was asking Lily about joining her shopping when they take Helen to Doc. Burn's office this morning. "I would love to Thelma, but I haven't any money."

Thelma burst into laughter before she answers. "Lily you are married to a very wealthy man. I'm sure my big brother will be accommodating." The two women laugh. Bradley was just entering the breakfast area where Lily and Thelma are.

He hears the woman laughing that was a good sign.   A quizzical look is on his face when he replies. "I see the two of you laughing, should I ask?"

Thelma brings Bradley up to speed about Lily going shopping when they take Helen to the Doctor. Bradley raises one quizzical brow at his wife, and sister. "Ok. That would be good for Lily show her our fair city.

"Lily darling you buy whatever you want, I will give you money after breakfast." Bradley sends his sister a silent thank you. Monica enters the area. She speaks to Bradley and Thelma, and totally ignores Lily.

Monica asks Thelma. "You want to do some shopping while were out with mother?" Thelma replies. "Yes and I invited Lily to join us." Monica turns to face Lily. "Oh, you are still here?" I thought you would have the decency to leave." Bradley's temper snaps. His eyes are cold as ice and he has a biting remark on his lips.

Chapter 4

Lily stops him. It was time she set the record straight. "Monica I'm truly sorry you don't like me and that is fine. However, I will not let you disrespect me or belittle me! I 'am your brother's wife like it or not!" Her silver eyes turn cold as winter.

Monica is no fool this was not the time or place. She would not rise to Lily's challenge, instead she submits for now. Her eyes shift in her brother's direction. His brows are drawn, and jaw clenched looking deadly.

It would not be wise to push Bradley at this moment; she tries to clean up the mess. "I shall not have my sister-in law angry with me, please forgive my behaviour." Lily did not buy Monica's apology, but it would do for now.

It was time to take Helen to see Doc. Burns. Everyone was ready and Bradley cools off enough to talk to his wife. "Enjoy yourself love. I have work to do! You and I need to talk about some things when you return."

She wants to ask about his last statement but there was not enough time. Instead, she hugs him and replies. "Ok love I will see you later."

St. Louis was big and beautiful! The streets lined with plenty of boutiques. The three women stroll through the shops, picking out lovely gowns, riding pants, and hats. It turns out to be a passable day.

When they return to the Doctor's office William informs them that they would be returning without Helen. "Your mother is going into in the hospital today." William was upset, but he takes the time to share with the women Helen's condition. He suggests they continue the conversation with the rest of the family.

Lily

The ride back to the ranch was in silence. The women and William enter the house as Brad was coming down the steps. His sharp eyes notice the expression on their faces. "Where is Mother?" He asks.

William answers the question. "Doc. Burns decided to admit her in the hospital. Son, collect your bothers, we will meet in the library. Bradley could see the strain on Williams face and does as asked. The whole family gathers in the library.

William starts the conversation. "I know we all are worried. The reason I asks you here is to tell you that Helen needs to have brain surgery. This procedure is very risky. We have to remain strong and pray your mother makes a swift recovery.

"Aaron speaks first. "Father, you don't have to worry about anything we will help you get through this." Daniel looks at Bradley he was always so calm and undaunted. Bradley rises from his seat and stands. He glances at his siblings faces before he speaks.

"William I will go with you to see mother this evening." Lily was by his side, her voice is a whisper. "I'm here if you need me." Bradley feels more confident that his mother would pull through with Lily by his side.

He holds Lily's hand before he excuses them both. Bradley was asking his wife to walk down to the stables with him. He needs to think, and it is urgent that he speak with Lily in private. Bradley is in conversation as he and Lily walk.

"Love, I need you to listen, and to please understand, I know, I promised you that we would return to Tennessee with your parents, but under the circumstances. My family needs me at this moment.

I 'am not sure if mother will pull through this, and my father depends on me to run his business." Lily listens quietly to his words. "My place is with you love. I understand." Bradley needs to tell her something else. He takes a deep breath and continues.

Lily

"There is another matter that requires my attention. We need more head of cattle, it is time to sell and buy, if my mother recovers. I have to go on a cattle drive in Texas, and it might be a month if not longer. Darling, I know this is a lot to tell you at once."

Lily smiles up at Bradley. "I will be fine but I will miss you terribly." He did not know what to expect when he broke the news, but he was so proud of her for understanding. "How did I get so lucky?" Lily smiles and hugs him. "I'm the one who is lucky to have a wonderful husband."

They continue walking further into a line of trees, which hides them from view. He kisses his wife unable to get enough of her. She was ravishing. He slides her dress off her shoulders, while she unfastens his pants. Their bodies entwine as one making passionate love on the soft grass.

A noise grabs his attention and quickly pulls his trousers on while Lily scrambles to her feet. When he scans the area, he catches the glimpse of a figure. It was coming closer toward them holding something in its hand.

Bradley immediately steps in front of Lily as if sensing danger. A short time later, the figure is in clear view. He lets out a round of curse words. "Oh my God, what in the hell is she doing here?" The person approaching them was Elaine.

His voice sounds cold, and devoid of emotion. "What the hell are you doing here Elaine?" She was a few feet away, and screams in outrage. "You're out here with your half-bred whore. I told you, you are mine."

Elaine begins running towards them at full speed. In a matter of seconds, she was upon them. Bradley was off guard, and did not see the knife in her hand. Elaine charges at Lily swinging the knife, barley missing her. Bradley moves in the middle to shield Lily from the attack.

Elaine changes direction and confronts Bradley wielding the knife at him as a maniac. Elaine was hell-bent on injuring Lily, but Bradley was blocking her path. Frustration enrages Elaine, and she turns the large knife on Bradley. She attacks Bradley with the knife swinging wildly as he ducks and moves out the way. She catches his forearm leaving an open gash. The sound of Lily's high-pitched scream slices the silence. She was terrified. Pain surges through his body and Bradley falls to the ground. The knife sliced into his forearm and blood was everywhere.

Bradley was bleeding heavily and recoils from the pain. Elaine smiles a wicked smile at Lily with Bradley injured there was no one to help, and sheer panic overtakes Lily. Elaine was walking towards Lily with a crazed look in her eyes. Lily froze with fear and her feet refuse to move. The woman is about to swing the knife at Lily once again.

A loud scream tears from Lily's throat, the sound echoes in the distance. She ducks the first blow, and Elaine returns for the second attempt. Lily glimpses Bradley on his feet. The next thing Lily saw was darkness.

Soft moans of pain shattered the silence as Lily stirs slightly. Her body ached, and her head was pounding like a drum. Bradley sits by her bedside for two days.

He was exhausted to a frazzle. Lily's eyes flutter, and slowly open. Confusion was on her face as she looks around the room. Her eyes settle on Bradley sitting in a chair with stubble on his chin. He looks exhausted. Bradley speaks first." Thank God! Hello love, I have been so worried about you."

Lily was struggling to sit up in the bed. "What happen?" The memory of what took place floods her mind, and she was afraid. Bradley senses her apprehension. "Calm down darling it is ok. You are safe!" "Where is Elaine?" Are you all right? I remember the knife and her swinging it towards you."

"It's just a scratch. I will be fine! Elaine is in a mental institution she clearly had a nervous mental breakdown. Daniel was taking a walk, and heard a woman's scream. He came to help me restrain Elaine, so I could bring you in the house.

You slipped on a rock, and hit your head. You are safe love." Lily breathes a sigh of relief, "How is Helen? Did the surgery go ok?" Bradley answers. "Mother is doing fine; she is still in the hospital recovering nicely."

"I am happy to hear that." She releases a drawn breath. Bradley did not want to tire his wife. "You need to build your strength my love." He offers his assistance with the soup then makes her rest. Lily agrees, she was still tired, and welcomes sleep. Bradley waits for a couple of minutes then leaves the room.

He was walking down the long hallway in search of his brothers. It was time to talk with Aaron, and Daniel about the cattle drive. The cattle drive would take place in a few weeks.

Daniel was on his way to the breakfast room. Bradley calls over to him. "Daniel, I need to speak with you and

Aaron." "Okay he should be down stairs shortly." Daniel waits for his brother to sit before asking.

"How is Lily?" "She is resting." Aaron was entering the room. He greets his brothers. "Good morning brothers and comments.

Bradley the argument between you and Elaine must have been one hell of one?"

The memory of what could have happen to him and Lily made his blood boil. No one could have told him Elaine was this disturbed. He pushes the thought from his mind and answers the question.

"It was! I told her about Lily and she lost control. I never thought she would try to harm Lily though." Bradley has a surprised look on his face. Daniel was paying attention to his brothers. Aaron replies. "What an unpleasant matter that had to be." Bradley raises his brow at his brother. "Yes it was, and one I won't forget soon."

Lily

He drops the conversation to keep his temper in check. The cattle drive was what he prefers to discuss, and he mentions the journey ahead of them.

You two realize this will be dangerous territory for all of us." William joins the men. "Good morning sons! How are you? What is this about?" Bradley responds. "Good morning father I'm making Daniel and Aaron aware of the danger we face on this cattle drive." William nods. "Very well, I would feel much better if you take a few more of the hands with you. Of course, I know you have your weapons." Daniel was eager. This was his first cattle drive, and the arrangements for the trip were complete.

Days turned into weeks. Helen was home fully recovered, and back to her old self everyone was relieved. William's attitude changed. He was cheerful and whistling these days. Lily regains her strength, and is practically back to her old self. The time was nearing for Bradley and his brothers to go on the cattle drive.

Lily and Helen walk down the stairs together with the rest of the family. Bradley strides toward his wife and mother. He kisses Helen on the forehead." Good day mother, are you feeling better?" Helen grins at her son. "I'm fine Bradley don't fuss son." Bradley walks over to his wife, and places a hand on the small of her back.

It was time to say his goodbyes. This was going to be a long departure, and he wants to hold on to his wife a little longer. Lily turns to face her husband. "I shall miss you love. I don't know what I shall do without you?" Light brown eyes twinkle at his wife. "I shall return to you Lily, there is nothing that could keep me away."

Brad hugs his wife closer, and eases away her fears. The men dressed in blue jeans chaps cover their pants, and revolver rest in the holster. Each man wears a ten-gallon hat that sits low on his heads. The top of their plaid shirts are unbutton at the throat.

Lily

Lily looks at her husband, and his graceful movements. She would recognize Bradley's stance from the others. He has a strength and grace that sets him apart from the rest of the group. She thought about his characteristics, the way his voice sounds like pure silk and the way he arch one brow when he was amused.

His face was the one she loved more than life itself. He jolts her out of her thoughts. "Walk with me Lily." They walk to the veranda as the men mount their horses. Bradley holds his Lily close. He bends his head to put a lingering kiss on her sweet lips.

A feeling of loneliness overcomes her, and tears run down her cheeks. The thought of a whole month or more without Bradley, was unbearable. "Don't cry darling. I will be back before you know I am gone." she musters a smile. "I love you, please be careful." Bradley stares deep into Lily's eyes. "I will!" He releases her, and mounts his stallion. The three brothers were on their journey.

Lily stands there watching until they disappear from sight. Helen was on the veranda waiting for Lily. She calls over to Lily. "Come here child sit with an old woman for a few minutes." Lily smiles, then turns toward the steps on the veranda. She sits with her on the porch. Helen explains to Lily the ways of a rancher's wife.

She goes into detail about her and William's struggle to keep their land. The land belonged to their parents, after years of saving every dime. "Lily, the reason I 'am telling you all of this, is to help you appreciate why Bradley is doing this. He wants to give the two of you a better life."

Lily thought over Helen words. "Thank you Helen, you are right." "Any time you need someone to talk to Lily, feel free. I'm here if you need me." She could smile now Helen explained a lot. "I will, I promise." Helen asks Lily for assistance climbing the stairs to her bedroom. She offers her support and guides Helen upstairs.

After she finishes her task, she decides to do a little reading, maybe that

Lily

would fill her time. It has been an hour since the men left, but seems like an eternity. Maybe a good book would help. Lily continues to the library, searching for any book one wants read. Thelma was just on her way out of the library when Lily arrives.

"I hope I haven't run you off." Lily asks. Thelma answers with a friendly smile. "Of course not I have been studying all day. I think I need a break." " Are you sure?" "Yes, see you later." Thelma was off. Lily settles down in one of the wing-backed chairs in front of the fireplace. She reads for a while, but her mind was on Bradley, wondering if he was safe.

She could not concentrate this evening. She leaves the library and walks outside on the veranda for a few minutes, staring at the night's sky. Lily was standing in the shadows, enjoying the cool breeze, but she was not alone. The sound of whispering voices surround her. At first, she thought she was hearing things. She strains her ears. She hears two people are talking.

It was a woman talking to a man. The woman was commenting. "How long do you expect me to keep up this pretence?" The man answers. "I know! You are going to have to be patient a little longer. You have my promise I will tell Helen soon, but now is not the time." The sound of the man's voice was familiar to Lily because it belongs to William.

The woman lets out a giggle. "I need you to hurry! I'm running out of time!" Lily decides she has heard enough of the conversation. She leaves the veranda, and her mind was reeling. She could not believe her ears. How could William, betray Helen like this?" She hurries into the house, and runs into Monica just as she was about to mount the stairs.

Monica stops Lily. "Have my brothers left yet?" Her reply was sharp, and abrupt. "Yes they left a couple hours ago!" Lily quickly mounts the stairs, leaving Monica staring after her.

Monica wonders what got into Lily. After she was in the bedroom, Lily paces the floor. She could not believe what she just witness, should she tell Bradley about this. Lily likes William, but after overhearing the conversation tonight, she suddenly has her doubts about him.

Bradley and his brothers settled down for the night. So far, the journey was progressing well. You could never be too careful out here this was still untamed country. Thieves and Indians roam free, and you never knew what to expect. Daniel decides to ask his brother for advice.

He approaches the conversation with Bradley. "Brad, how did you know that you were in love with Lily?" Bradley raises one quizzical brow at his younger brother. He hesitates before answering because he was not sure where this question was leading. There was something different about Daniel, his personality changed.

Bradley thinks on Daniels question for a few moments, and decides to find out what was bothering his brother. The question heightens his curiosity, and he wonders what brought this on.

"I knew that I was in love with Lily the very first time I saw her. You get a feeling that makes you all twisted inside. You have a hunger that is never satisfied. Why do you ask?" Daniel thought over Brad's words before he replies. Aaron was listening to his brothers' conversation.

Daniel builds his courage before answering. "I met a woman; well let's say I have known her for some time. I want to ask for her hand in marriage." Aaron sits up to hear more clearly. Bradley is gazing at his younger brother with a penetrating stare. "I must ask you again Daniel what brought this on.

Furthermore why haven't you mentioned this to Aaron or me before?" Daniel shrugs his wide shoulders. "The reason I haven't mentioned her to the family is because I figure no one would approve. I have finally found someone that I love."

Aaron puts his two-cent in. "The thought of settling down has crossed my mind also." Aaron is looking at both his brothers. Bradley admits Aaron was serious.

"Then all I can say to you too is congratulations.

The three men decide to make it a night. There are several more days of hard ridding ahead. Days turn into weeks. Bradley's mind was constantly on Lily. How he misses her, but he also knows he has to keep his mind clear so they could return home safely.

Bradley and his men were gone over four weeks, and he was dearly missing Lily. So far, the trip was going well. Texas was hot and women were readily available, but Bradley was not interested. His mind was focus on business and a speedy return home.

Daniel and Aaron were settling in for the night. Bradley for some odd reason could not sleep. It was as if he was on guard. Aaron asks. "What do you think Brad? So far, so good, hopefully we will get back without a scratch." Brad glances at his brother with a concerned stare. "I hope so Aaron."

Bradley sits on the ground, and places his rifle next to him before settling back against a tree. No matter how hard he tries, a sense of uncertainty overcomes him. Bradley could not shake the uneasy feelings. When he wakes, it was to the sound of his men yelling Indians. Brad and his brothers are on their feet with guns in hand.

Brad must have dosed off a few minutes, but his mind was alert, and ready for whatever. There were Indians on palominos some had war paint on their faces. The Indian with the large crown of feathers waves Bradley to come closer. Brad is sure he was their chief.

Bradley knows that they are outnumbered, and he asks his men to hold their fire. He stands to his full height, and bravely walks closer to the chief. Surprisingly he speaks English. The chief informs Bradley they were entering Indian Territory, and he explains for Bradley and his men to cross cost ten head of cattle.

Bradley considers the chiefs words, it seems like a fair trade. The chief was offering to escort Bradley and his men through the rough terrain. Bradley thanks the chief, and turns to leave. The chief stops him. He signals one of his warriors to bring forth a squaw.

The chief spoke in his language and the squaw came forward. The chief informs Bradley that her name is Moon and she is a gift to them. Bradley is wise enough not to refuse the offer of the squaw; it would be an insult to the chief, and he accepts the woman as a gift.

True to the chief's word, the warriors safely escort Bradley and his men through the rough terrain. Once the chief and his men separate, Bradley wonders how he was going to explain the woman to Lily. Meanwhile Lily tries to get through the long days and the even longer nights.

She avoids William as much as possible. After witnessing his betrayal, she was uncomfortable around him. There was a letter waiting for Lily, and Thelma hands it to her. It was from Bradley, explaining they should be home in two weeks.

Chapter 5

Lily was anticipating her husband's return. She was surprised how slow the mail was as she walks to the veranda the three men were ridding up on their horses. Bradley and his men returned home safely with the cattle they went after. Lily runs into Bradley's strong arms.

She was breathless her hair was pulled into a ponytail, and she was lovely. Bradley did not waste any time. He dismounts and enfolds his wife into his arms. The kiss he places on her lips was long and passionate, and promises passion later.

Bradley lifts his head to look into her lovely face, before he speaks. "Hello love, I have missed you! We have many things we need to discuss, and my hope is that you understand." Lily was excited. "Whatever it is, it doesn't matter Bradley.

You are home, that is what matters." Bradley hugs his wife closer, maybe she would understand. Meanwhile Aaron and Moon have been getting close. Brad is aware that Aaron has taken a fancy to Moon. As far as he could tell, she feels the same way about him.

Daniel on the other hand is acting strange. He is preoccupied with something, not talking much and acting withdrawn. He was walking up to Bradley and Lily. "I will tell mother and father that we have a guest with us. Then without another word, he leaves. Moon and Aaron were walking towards the back of the house.

Aaron was falling for Moon. She was fluent in English and Moon describes her life living among her tribe, it was fascinating. She was friendly and beautiful not like the women Aaron was use to in their fancy clothes sharing the latest gossip. She was more down to earth, and has values.

They sit on a bench in his mother's flower garden, talking for hours about their similar qualities. It was at that point in time Aaron realizes she is the one for him. He decides at that moment, he has to have her in his life. He slips her hand in his, and they are staring at each other. Aaron was not going to let this moment pass.

He leans forward and places a light kiss on her lips. Moon feels the warmth of his lips on hers, and tingles shoot through her body. Her pulse quickens and she returns his kiss with enthusiasm.

"I love your home it is so peaceful." Aaron was staring at Moon with open desire, and she returns his stare. She was assessing him. His lips are full, and his complexion a caramel color. His body strong and physically perfect with an athletic build, and his hair is neat and wavy. Aaron was a very good-looking man. The attraction was mutual.

When she looks in his direction, their eyes make contact once more. Aaron leans over, and draws Moon into his arms. The kiss between them is deep and passionate. Aaron was breathing fast she stirs his senses; it was something he has not felt in a long time. He compliments Moon in every way possible.

Moon never dreamed her life would take such a dramatic turn, being with Aaron made her heart fill with happiness. Aaron clears his throat before asking his next question. "Moon, I am not very good at this, but my love and desire for you will not let me wait. Would you consider marrying me, I could provide a good life for the both of us."

She is about to answer, but nervousness drives Aaron on. "At least think about it. This is the first time in my life that I have ever wanted to share my life with someone."

Moon is still holding his hand in hers, this was the sweetest confession she has ever heard. The expression on her face is warm, and she tilts her head to look him in the eye. When she answers, she sounds breathless. "Yes I will marry you Aaron.

The feeling is mutual, and I knew you were the one for me as soon as I lay eyes on you."

Aaron is ecstatic; he was silently holding his breath. This time he pulls Moon on her feet, and holds her in his arms promising a life she deserves. As an afterthought, he mentions to Moon that they need to tell his family, so they could share in their happiness.

William and Helen wait patiently for Bradley to enter the house. Helen was the first to reply. "Thank God for your safe return. I 'am grateful for all of my son's safety." Bradley walks over, and hugs his mother. He places a kiss on her forehead. William replies. "Well son I'm glad you had a good trip. I would like to talk about it in detail after dinner, if you're not too tired?"

"Of course William, it will have to wait until later. Right now I want to freshen up and spend a few minutes with my wife." William is aware of the snub. "Very well son of course I understand." There has always been a battle of wills between the two men, even though they love each other.

Lily

Bradley picks Lily up and climbs the stairs two at a time. She was all giggles. After they reach their room, he lowers his wife placing her feet on the ground. Then he mentions Moon and Aaron. He explains how the tribe traded Moon, and his brother's infatuation with her.

He cuts the explanations short because his desire intensifies when he glances at his wife. "Enough about them, your husband is in need of his wife." He was undressing Lily, and she feels his strong hands caress her soft skin.

His tongue slides across her full breast as his hands cup each one. The palm of his hands caresses her backside. Lily feels the firmness of him against her thigh, and she reveals in the knowledge that she entices him beyond reason.

Brad bends his head lower moving his mouth over each breast catching the nubs between his teeth. Then she feels his warm mouth causing a vacuum effect as he suckles her breast. A groan of delight escapes her lips. Brad moves his hands over her body with expertise. Using his experience, he touches her in the right places. Lily puts her hands over his shoulders then along his back. She was massaging his buttocks. It makes him explode with pleasure.

He coos his wife, and then asks. "Lily what are you doing to me? I want you more and more." The confession from her husband gives Lily a sense of power, and she loves it. After the lovemaking, they join the rest of the family in the dining room.

Monica and Thelma were talking with Moon. She was a beauty with her waist length hair, soft brown eyes, and soft voice. Lily and Moon hit it off right away. Lily notice the secrete look's between Aaron and Moon. Daniel on the other hand was moody.

He stands taping his glass to get everyone's attention. "I have some news that I would like to share with the family." Bradley was paying close attention. Daniel pauses, to glance at Bradley first. "I guess you think I have been acting strange brother. "I want you to know that I have asked a young lady for her hand, in marriage, and she accepts."

Bradley was about to congratulate Daniel, but he continues. The woman was waiting outside the door. She could hardly wait to see the look on Bradley's face. Daniel was walking towards the door. "The woman I want to marry is waiting outside the door."

Daniel opens the door and the woman steps inside the room; everyone at the table is speechless. The woman was Elaine. After the shock wears off, Bradley's temper explodes. Helen was the first to ask. "Daniel is this some kind of sick joke." "I assure you mother this is no joke. Elaine is with child and it is mine! We are going to wed!"

Helen was in shock. She looks at William, and he returns her stare, and tries to explain. "I was going to tell you myself, Daniel insist that he should be the one to tell you. I have carried his secret to long."

Lily abruptly jumps to her feet, as tears run down her face. She runs away from the table this was too much for her to bear. Thelma and Moon were in pursuit after her. Elaine was gloating, with a look of complete satisfaction.

She still wants Bradley! It did not matter if she has to settle for Daniel. It was a small price to pay, as long as she was close to Bradley. The look Bradley gives Elaine was one of pure disgust. Monica was sitting back enjoying her brothers predicament.

Bradley takes one look at his sister, and confirms what he was thinking. He abruptly leaves the table, and his brows are together with anger. The expression on his face was dangerous. The liquid gold of his eyes turn darker, he was murderously angry. As he pauses to talk with Daniel, his voice was tight with emotion.

"I will talk to you later on this subject." Aaron knows Brad was trying to contain his anger. Without a backwards glance, Bradley excuses himself from the table. He went in search of Lily. Helen and

Lily

William were at odds; it seems everyone lost their appetite. Thelma and Moon are looking after Lily.

They get her to calm down. Thelma feels bad for her brother, and Lily they have been through so much. After Bradley enters the room, he asks Moon and Thelma to leave so he could talk to his wife.

"Lily darling, I don't like this any more than you. I know that my parents are not happy about the situation either. Right now, they have no choice. They will not turn Elaine away while she is with child."

It was her turn to talk. "Bradley, I understand, but I don't trust that woman, after all she tried to kill us." "You have my word love, I will not let any harm come to you darling." She buries her face in his chest. She knew this was true. "Sweetheart, try and get some rest I will be back shortly. There are a couple of things I need to discuss with my father and brothers."

Brad places a light kiss on his wife's lips and quietly leaves the room. He strolls into the library. Aaron, Daniel, and William are waiting for him to make an appearance. William replies. "Bradley, I know you and Lily have a problem with this matter, so does the rest of the family."

Bradley was sarcastic, "is that what you call this William?" Aaron feels it is time to intervene. This difference of opinion could turn into a battle of wills. "Look you two this is not the time.

We have to figure out a way to help Daniel right now." The two men agree for the moment, and turn their attention to Daniel. "There is nothing to help with. I love Elaine, and she loves me! We will be wed and that is the end of it!"

Daniel was not going to budge. Bradley could remain silent no longer. "I have to disagree with you Daniel. How do you know this is your child? You know Elaine has mental problems! Have you even considered what you are getting into?" Daniel's temper flares. "Who are you to question Elaine's moral character?

Lily

You dumped her for Lily! Oh, yes big brother Elaine told me all about it. And for your information we have been lovers ever since you went to Tennessee." Bradley could not believe this was his little brother speaking to him this way. Brads eyes are slits, his jaw hard and unrelenting.

"I will tell you this only once Daniel. Elaine is trouble and you do not have my approval." William glances between his two sons. He hates what was happening here. Daniel walks to the door, and replies. "Bradley, I think we have said all we need to say."

Aaron was pouring the three of them a stiff drink. Brad sits in silence for a moment. After he gulps down the drink, he refills his glass. William comments to Bradley. "Son, you're too hard on yourself, Daniel will find his way." Bradley nods in agreement. In a clipped voice, he replies. "You are right William."

William bids his son's goodnight, and hugs them both before making his departure. Aaron approaches Bradley. He was pouring another drink. "Easy on that, you need to have your wits about you right now! You better watch your step especially with Elaine in our home." Brad knows Aaron was right, but so much has happened.

He wonders when things will calm down enough to share Lily and his plans. "Don't worry Aaron, I will be fine." Aaron was not so sure, but he says his goodnights, and then exits the room. Bradley sits there for about an hour still drinking and staring into the fireplace.

A feeling of restless overtakes him. He leaves the library and goes to check on Lily. She was sleeping peacefully, and he walks down the hallway to the stairs. He decides to take a ride on his horse. Bradley continues walking to the stables. It was late and he has been drinking, but that did not deter him. The nights air was cool on Brad's skin it was refreshing.

He rides his horse fast and hard for an hour or more then returns to the stables. After he removes, the saddle from the horse, he rubs him down for the night. He continues to walk in the direction of the house, and notices a light on when he enters the foyer. He glimpses a shadow moving in the library, and hears footsteps, thinking it was Lily up reading a book he follows the sound.

Bradley enters the room, and steps towards the high back chair. He whispers calling to Lily, but no answer. He walks over to the front of the chair, but it was not Lily sitting there. It was Elaine. She has a see through gown on, and rushes to her feet, after noticing Bradley about to leave.

In a breathless voice, she stops him. "Wait, Bradley, please don't go! I want to talk." His face was set in stone, and his golden eyes are cold. "I have nothing to talk to you about Elaine." Elaine seizes the moment, and places her arms around Bradley's waist. She molds her body against his. It was time to seduce Bradley with her womanly charms.

She grinds her hips against his manhood. In a rhythmic motion, she continues slowly grinding her body against him. She tilts her lips towards his mouth, and kisses him with passion. Her tongue slips between his mouth circling between his teeth, and her hands slowly caress his manhood with deliberate purpose. Bradley was feeling the effects of the liquor.

The liquor intensifies his need. He was feeling the blood rush into his loins; in his drunken state, he lost the battle of the flesh. Elaine was an expert at seduction, and Bradley was under her spell. He was touching her breast drawing each one to his lips. He lowers his head to suckle them until the nipples were erect.

Elaine lets out moans of pleasure, feeling his hands on her flesh once more. She could feel the strength in his hands, as he touches her in intimate places. Elaine draws Bradley down to the floor, and lowers his pants. Once on top of him, her hands guide his swollen manhood into her core.

Once inside she rides him at a fevered pitch, her body bouncing up and down. The movements are slow and deliberate suiting her purpose, and she could not get enough of him. Elaine's mouth opens, to release a gasp of sexual gratification. She moans. "Oh, Bradley I missed your touch, and having you next to me."

Bradley was oblivious to Elaine. The next thing Bradley hears is the door to the library, as it swings open. Standing in the doorway was Daniel, and his face twisted with anger. He was furious. Elaine scrambles away. Bradley staggers when he tries to pull up his pants, before he knows it, Daniel hits him. Bradley and Daniel were tussling on the floor. Elaine screams! William, Aaron, and Lily enter the room.

William and Aaron separate the two men. Lily notes the gown Elaine was wearing. She has no doubt, what has taken place in the room. William is yelling! "Daniel, what the hell is going on in here?" Daniel is out of breath, but he regains his composer. "Why don't you tell everybody what's going on Bradley? Why don't you explain this situation especially to your wife?"

Bradley was dazed from all the alcohol. His light brown eyes lock with grey. Bradley stumbles to his feet, and walks over to Lily. "I can explain. This is not what it seems, Elaine seduced me. I had too much to drink. There was a loud noise in the room after Lily smartly slaps Bradley across the cheek, and he reaches up touching the area still stinging from the blow. Bradley stands there in shock.

Lily struck him. Her eyes were blazing, and her voice was firm. "I will be returning to my parents tomorrow." She spun on her heel and left without a backwards glance. Elaine rushes over to Daniel. She was lying to him about Bradley forcing himself on her. She exaggerates about coming to the library to read a book.

Daniel believes every word. Bradley hears the lies. It takes only a second before he explodes with a roar. "You bitch, you seduced me. I want you the hell out of this house." Aaron and William look at each other they both are aware that Elaine was going to be trouble for their family.

Lily

Bradley spends the night sleeping on a couch. He was tortured all night long with his betrayal of Lily. He thinks to himself. *Oh God, what have I done?* It was early in the morning hours when sleep comes to Bradley.

Lily flops across the bed, and cries herself to sleep. She was tortured with images of Elaine making love to her husband, and the smile on her face when Lily entered the room.

Morning arrives. William brings Helen up to speed about last night's episode. Helen was upset. "I cannot sit here and let Elaine destroy our family William. I want you to ask her and Daniel to leave." William replies. "I will have a talk with Daniel this morning." Lily sits on the bed that she spent so many months with Bradley.

Her eyes swollen from crying all night, she feels as if the bottom has fallen out of her world. She begins to pack her clothes, and debate if she should ask Aaron to purchase a ticket for her return home. Just as she was putting her, last item in her suitcase.

There was a light tap at her door. Bradley was standing there looking as if he has not slept. Lily opens the door wider for him to enter the room. He starts the conversation. "Lily, I can stand here and give you one million reasons how I wish this never happened. I know it will not take the hurt away that I caused you. However I do believe you know how very much I love you."

She holds her chin high, and faces Bradley head on. "Bradley you have disgraced me before your whole family. You have betrayed my trust. I don't think I can forgive that." Bradley placed his hands on Lily's shoulders. She flinches, as if he disgusts her. Bradley became angry, not with Lily but himself.

His light brown eyes turn hard, and his face was stone. When he replies it was in a harsh tone. "Look into my eyes and tell me, you love me no more Lily." Lily raises her eyes to meet Bradley. She answers stiffly. "I love you no more." Bradley was crushed, to hide his hurt he replies in a savage voice." I will have Aaron purchase your ticket for your return home. Goodbye Lily."

Bradley turns on his heel and walks out of the room. On the inside, his breath was gone; it takes all his strength to walk away from her. Lily stares after him with tears rolling down her cheeks. William, Daniel and Aaron were in the study. William is ready to approach Daniel about last night. "Daniel, I'm afraid you and Elaine will have to leave my home."

Daniel turns on William. "Your home, what about my home father this is about Brad isn't it?" William was angry now. "Son Bradley might be a lot of things, but I know he never took advantage of Elaine. She was after Bradley from the very start." Aaron joins William.

"Daniel she is using you! She lied about Bradley. I know first-hand Bradley had a few to many drinks, but he would never take advantage of her." Daniel has to admit they were right. He even accepts it. "You are right. I took Elaine away from here this morning. She confessed that she lied! It was all to hurt Bradley and Lily.

When I confronted her about the pregnancy, and Bradley she laughed in my face. She confessed to me that there never was a child. I feel like a complete fool." Bradley enters the room. Daniel feels awful about the fight with Bradley. His golden eyes were hard. "Good morning. Aaron, I need you to purchase a ticket for Lily's return home."

Aaron's head snaps up at the request. He was staring at his brother wondering if he has taken leave of his senses. "You mean to tell me you are going to let her just leave?"

Brad replies, "Lily told me she loves me no more. It is over!" Aaron saw pain in his brother's face. Daniel was speaking to Brad. "Brother I want to apologize for hitting you. I am sorry you were right the whole time about Elaine. I'm sorry for the pain I have caused you."

Lily

Bradley listens to his younger brothers words, but he was hurting right now. "I tried to warn you about Elaine, but you wouldn't listen. Now my wife is leaving me. Give your apology to someone else I will not forgive you Daniel." William intervenes. "Son, you have to go after your wife. You can't just give up, and don't be a stubborn fool."

Thelma, Moon and Helen try as hard as they can to get Lily to stay, but her pride was injured and her mind made up. Aaron bought the ticket for Lily. She hugs Helen and William thanking them for their hospitality. Bradley stands in the distance watching as his wife prepares to depart.

Chapter 6

Helen came to him earlier, she pleads with him to go after his wife, but his pride got the better of him. He would watch her go. Bradley follows the coach to the train station to make sure Lily was safe. He looks from a distance. Lily hugs Thelma and Moon "I shall miss you two terribly." "We shall miss you also Lily."

Aaron places money in Lily's hand. "Take this Lily, it's from Bradley." Lily was about to give the money back to Aaron, however, he insisted. Aaron replies. "Take the money Lily you will need it."

Aaron stares at Lily for a moment feeling dreadful when he sees the hurt in her eyes. He runs a hand across his neck and replies. "My brother will not let you go. I know that Bradley loves you, and he will come around."

Lily

Lily hugs Aaron crying the whole time. "Thank you Aaron, goodbye." She was on the train for the long ride home. Bradley watches his Lily go. He rides his horse hard and fast back to the house. Bradley enters the house, slams the door, and climbs the steps two three at a time. He enters what use to be Lily and his room. Bradley stands with fist clenched, and scans the room.

The scent of Lily's perfume still lingers in the air, and the memory torments him. He was like a wounded animal. Damn he missed her already, what was he going to do? Lily did not notice the scenery her heart was heavy. Her mind was a constant replay of Elaine with Bradley. She groans in agony. Fresh tears begin to fall from her eyes.

After a few days ride Lily was at the train station and her parents were eagerly waiting for her. Her father helps with the luggage. Margarita was smiling. "Lily my sweet child, I have missed you." Lily runs into her mother's arms seeking comfort. She tightly holds on to her mother and tears fall like rain.

Thomas has his suspicions something was amiss, when he received the telegram from Bradley. It said that Lily was coming for a visit. Thomas was looking at the state his daughter was in, and he becomes angry.

Margarita calms and soothes Lily. Thomas helps his wife and daughter in the buggy. They were on their way home. Margarita did not press Lily for details she wants her to settle down first, there was plenty of time to talk. After arriving at their home Lily notices, the new room addition to the house, there was a new piano also.

Lily asks. "Father you have been renovating." Thomas grins. "Yes thanks to your husband. Bradley helped me find buyers for my crops." Margarita shows Lily to her room. The room was freshly painted and new furniture added. The house really looks lovely. ." Margarita was saying.

"You need to rest after your long journey! We'll talk later." "I am a little tired mother. Thank you." Margarita makes her exit so Lily could rest. It gives her and

Thomas time to try and figure out what was going on with Bradley and Lily. Thomas was saying.

"Now, Margarita, don't get yourself in a hiss, it is probably a lover's quarrel we have had our share." Margarita was smiling, and replies. "You are probably right Thomas."

Lily's head hit the pillow and she was asleep. She was tired a lot lately, and hungry. Days turn into weeks since her departure. Bradley would scan the mail secretly hoping for a letter from Lily, after none came he becomes unbearable. The men are afraid to ask him a question twice.

Bradley worked long hours and goes on every cattle drive. His family watches as he works himself into a tired stupor. Aaron, Daniel, and William decide they should have a talk with Bradley. His workers were complaining, and his family witness the change in him.

William approaches Bradley one morning. "Brad I need to speak with you its most urgent." "Not now William. I have a cattle drive to get ready for." William was firm. "No! Now Bradley" Bradley raises one brow at his father. He knows William was not going to bend.

"Very well William." He follows his father to the library, and Aaron and Daniel were present. William starts the conversation. "Your workers are complaining of unfair treatment by you." Bradley raises one brow at William his light brown eyes dangerously cold.

"I will not have you questioning my authority! You put me in charge of these operations. If the hands have a complaint then they need to bring it to my attention." Williams temper snaps. "Dam it son, you're hurting right now, we all know this! You can't keep punishing yourself and everyone around you."

Aaron saw the look on Bradley's face, and he knows a storm is brewing. Aaron tries to help the situation. "Bradley, I know you are in love with Lily, and she is still in love with you. Swallow your pride and bring your wife home." Bradley turns on his family; he was trying to forget Lily.

Every time he thought he was numb, someone would just reopen his wound. His tone is sharp. "You know no such thing. I will not discuss Lily. For the love of God do not mention her name again." Brad picks up his hat, puts it on top his head, and strolls out the room.

Aaron would not let Brad off that easy. He catches up with him. "Bradley, I spoke with Lily at the train station. She is still in love with you, and if you let her get away that makes you a fool." Bradley faces Aaron. He could not fool Aaron. "I have tried to get Lily to stay, but she loves me no more."

Aaron hears the pain and sadness in his brother's voice. Aaron replies. "That is anger and hurt talking Bradley! She is hurting two! If anyone deserves to be together it's you two." Bradley lets his guard down with Aaron admitting he was right. Aaron hugs his brother. "You, think on my words Brad."

Lily misses Bradley more and more she still has not heard from him. She is ready to talk to her mother about her breakup with Bradley.

Margarita listens to Lily, and then she asks. "Dear I'm not making excuses for Bradley, but sometimes men do strange things. You say that he was drinking! Maybe, this woman took advantage of that fact.

Lily is this worth your marriage. Only you can make that decision." Lily was gaining weight, and being ill in the mornings. Finally, Margarita informs Lily. "You're with child that is why you are always hungry and ill in the mornings.

You have to write Bradley and let him know." Thomas was happy to hear he would be a grand pa, but he was concerned about Lily's marriage.

Lily

It has been two months now and no Bradley. Moon and Aaron announce their wedding date. They want Lily present. Moon sends a telegram to Lily inviting her, and her family. Aaron goes to tell Bradley about the telegram. "Brad I want you to hear this from us.

Moon and I have invited Lily to the wedding. I hope this is good news for you?" For the first time in a while, Bradley smiles. "This is very good news. Do you think she will come?" Aaron replies. "Let's hope so."

Lily receives the telegram about Moon and Aaron's wedding. She already mailed a letter to Bradley expressing she needs to see him. She secretly hopes that Bradley is still in love with her.

She thinks about him every night and day. Bradley, Aaron, and Moon were on the veranda when the mail was coming in.

Bradley strolls off the veranda to get the mail. He was reading a letter it was from Lily. Bradley was rushing up the stairs of the veranda. Moon and Aaron saw him smiling. Aaron asks. "Is everything alright Brad?" Brad replies while handing Aaron the letter.

"Better than alright" "Were you going Brad?" Aaron asks. Bradley was smiling ear to ear. "I am going to bring my wife home." "Thank God." Aaron replies. Bradley runs up the stairs. He packs his clothes and a pistol. He mounts his stallion, and on the way to Tennessee. It was colder now, the air was crisp, and Lily is still waiting for Bradley to reply to her letter.

She is unsure how he will take the news. Would he still want her? She stands by her favourite tree facing the front of her and Thomas fishing hole. Lily was leaning against the tree when she hears footsteps. Lily thought it was Thomas or Margarita coming to fetch her.

When she turns to look in the direction of the footsteps, she was staring into light brown eyes. "Hello, love. I have been missing you." Bradley walks closer to Lily. Her heart was beating fast. "Hello,

Bradley. I have missed you also." Bradley pulls Lily close to his heart.

"I have been so miserable without you, Lily my love. I was a stubborn fool." Bradley leans down to place a kiss on her lips. She lifts her mouth to receive him, and their world was right once more. "I was so afraid that you would not come." "Nothing could keep me away Lily. I love you."

Lily breathes a sigh of relief. "I have something to tell you. I'm with child." Bradley holds Lily at arm's length. His light brown eyes bore into hers. "Are you sure?" Lily nods. Then Bradley picks Lily up and swings her around. He was laughing. "This is wonderful news. Are you ok with this?"

Lily was smiling. "Bradley how could I not be okay, this is our child, a part of you and me. I couldn't be happier." Bradley kisses Lily long on her lips. She places her hand in his and they walk back to her parent's home. Once inside Thomas and Bradley begin making plans.

Thomas was talking to Bradley after the women left the room. "Bradley I'm glad you and Lily have worked things out. I was getting worried. What are we going to do about the house for Lily and you?" Bradley ponders the question. "I would like to start building on the house now! That way it will be ready for Lily and the baby.

My brother is to be wed I would be honored if you and Margarita join us for the happy occasion." Now it was Thomas turn to pause for a minute. "We would not want to be a bother for your family. You and Lily have just reconciled." Bradley interrupts.

"Nonsense, my family would be pleased to meet Lily's parents. I will not take no for an answer! Thomas you two have been very kind to me." Thomas admits he was at a loss, so he accepts the invitation. "Good." Bradley was satisfied, he would telegram his family and let them know that they all would be arriving in a few days' time.

Thomas assures Bradley the building of the house would take place as soon as he and Margarita return home. Bradley was satisfied with their agreement. It was time to join Lily and her mother. The men share their plans with the women. Lily and Margarita were very happy with the news.

Preparations are complete for Moon and Aaron's wedding. The telegram from Bradley arrive a couple of days ago, and they have the guest bedrooms ready for Lily, and her parent's arrival. Bradley, Thomas, Lily, and Margarita all board the train. They should be arriving in a few days' time.

William and Helen look forward to meeting Lily's parents, and pray this wedding would bring them all a little closer. Aaron and Daniel go to meet Bradley and Lily's parents at the train station. Bradley introduces Aaron and Daniel to Lily's parents. Aaron extends his hand to Thomas who shakes both men's hand.

Aaron was making idle conversation with Lily's parents. "It is a pleasure to finally meet you both. I see where Lily gets her good looks." Aaron's last comment directed to Margarita, and a blush creeps across her cheeks. "It is nice to meet you." Margarita replies. Thomas stakes his claim. "You are so right! That is why she's the love of my life."

Aaron surprised by Thomas stern declaration, and he shifts his glance at Bradley, hoping he did not offend Thomas. Thomas smiles at the younger man's confusion. "Don't worry young fellow no harm done." This time they all laugh, and enjoy the long ride to the Thomas household. Helen and William greet Lily, and her parents with a warm welcome.

Their parents sit down to get to know each other better, Helen and Margarita became inseparable. William and Thomas both have a lot in common. The two men agree on a little fishing before Thomas leaves. Helen shows Margarita the grounds and the entire house from top to bottom.

Margarita was very impressed. Tomorrow was Aaron's big day. Aaron, Daniel, and Bradley are in the library, and

Bradley takes this opportunity to share the good news with his brothers.

"Well, brothers it is my pleasure to inform you that Lily is with child, and I could not be more pleased." Aaron and Daniel both congratulate Brad's good fortune. Daniel replies. "I'm going to be an uncle. I like that." A smile touches his lips.

Aaron was happy about the news. "Have you told mother, and William?" Brad replies. "Not yet, I was planning on informing them at dinner. It will give me the opportunity to share our good news with the family."

Aaron replies. "Then shall we be on our way." The family gathers at the dinner table. The cooks perform an exceptional job with the meal. Everything smells delicious.

Thelma and Monica were in conversation with Lily's parents. Bradley glances over at his wife. She nods her approval, and Bradley stands raising his glass for a toast.

"A toast to Aaron, and Moon may their life together be full of happiness. Please raise your glasses once more, to my beautiful wife Lily, who will soon be the mother of my child? I could not be happier."

Everyone raises his or her glass, and supply warm congratulations, including Monica. Dinner was a success. The men retire to the library, and the women to the parlour. Moon, Thelma, Monica, and Helen were congratulating Lily. Margarita was happy to see the kindness the family was displaying towards her daughter.

After a couple of hours, the women decide they should rest up. After all tomorrow was the wedding. Lily walks with her mother and Helen towards their rooms. Bradley steps inside the room where Lily was. "Hello, love. I want to make sure you are ok. Do you need anything?"

Lily looks at her husband with love in her eyes. "No Bradley I'm fine. I am going to rest for a while." Tiredness was winning the battle with Lily, she yawns. "I am a little tired." Bradley brushes his lips against his wife. "If you need me I will be in library with the men, were playing poker for a while. I'm not far." Lily knows Bradley wants to join the men.

She hurries him along. "You go on have yourself some fun. I will be fine." Bradley quietly closes the door, and makes his way to the card game. Thomas was a very good card player, but so was William. The men have brandy and cigars. The topic of the conversation was business.

"William this is a very large piece of land." Thomas was saying. William responds. "We will have to go riding tomorrow, so I can show you all of it. Daniel and Aaron join the card game. Bradley was joking with the two older men." So what do you two think about being grandpa's?" William and Thomas look at each other, and smile. "Were just fine with it aren't we William."

William agrees gingerly. Then the laughter ends, and a serious look is on William's face. He directs his question to Bradley. "Thomas was informing me that you and Lily are having a home built in Tennessee. When were you planning to tell us?" Bradley light brown eyes meet his father's stern ones. "I was planning to tell you, and mother months ago. It has been so crazy around here these past months."

William continues. "I knew one day you would have a family of your own son. Hell, all of you one day will be gone. That is why I have pushed you, and your brothers, so hard to learn the business. I don't want you to have to struggle like me, and your mother did." Bradley finds a new respect for William. It was the first time in his life that William opens up to them.

"Thank, you father. I hope you are satisfied, and proud." William replies. "You all have made me proud son." After many hours of cards, the men say their goodnights. The guests are arriving for the ceremony at the ranch. The priest arrives. Thomas and Margarita are in their Sunday's best.

The rest of William's family is present. The Thomas brothers wore tailored suits. Lily admires her husband in his formal attire he looks so very handsome. Lily was as eye catching as ever in her chiffon dress. The women all wore matching outfits, but Lily still stands out in the crown. Bradley glances over at his wife, and a feeling of pride courses through him.

Moon enters the room, and William is by her side. She was lovely. Her hair circles her beautiful face with spiral curls. The back of her hair was upswept in a French twist.

Aaron has no doubts this was the right woman for him. He accesses his wife's lovely features, as the priest reads their vows. Moon was stunning in her silk white dress.

Everyone cries, and hugs them both. The music is playing in the background, and fancy champagne glasses are over flowing with expensive champagne, everyone was enjoying this blessed union. Bradley hugs, Moon, and congratulates Aaron.

It was time to locate his wife. Bradley separates from the group, and walks in Lily's direction to ask for a dance. There was a younger man speaking with Lily. The younger man seems to be very interested in her. Bradley feels a tinge of anger mounting.

The man was just a little too taken with his wife, and he quickens his steps. Once he was close to Lily and the young man. He interrupts the conversation in a smooth voice "Hello love, may I have the pleasure of a dance with my lovely wife?"

Bradley's expression clearly initiates a challenge. His eyes shift toward the other man. Lily was unaware of the admiring looks from the men in the room, and she pays no mind.

A sound of delight accompanies a brilliant smile as she lovingly glances at her husband. "Of course, I would love to dance with my husband." She pauses for one moment. "Bradley let me introduce you to Randall Johnson. He is a rancher also." Bradley grips the other man's hand in a firm handshake.

Lily

The younger man was saying. "It's good to meet you Bradley. I have heard many brave stories about you sir." Bradley was dissecting the man with his eyes. "Thank you, but don't believe everything you hear. Now if you will excuse me sir. I would love the pleasure of my wife's company."

The man named Randall expression changes. He is a bit cross with Bradley for dismissing him. It was okay one day it would be him doing the dismissing. "Of course, please forgive me." Bradley guides Lily to the grand floor, and waltzes like an expert with her.

He lowers his voice then asks. "Who is this Randall Johnson?" Lily notes anger in Brad's voice. She lifts her head to look into his eyes. "I truly don't know love. He just came over, and introduced himself. Is something wrong?" Bradley admits he was over reacting.

When he replies, it was with a smile, and his facial expression is calm. "There is nothing wrong sweetheart, nothing at all."

The night was full with laughter, music, food, and song. Helen and William are waltzing together, and so are Thomas and Margarita.

Aaron and Moon glow with happiness, and are inseparable. Monica and Thelma have the pleasure of meeting the Johnson brothers. Both women are smitten with the two brothers.

Randall Johnson and his brother Luke are on the prowl. The plan was to be better acquainted with Thelma and Monica.

Chapter 7

If everything goes as plan this would be a breeze. Moon and Aaron are ready to depart. They were spending their honeymoon traveling in Europe.

The guests are thinning out. Thelma and Monica are still in conversation with the Johnson brothers. Daniel was dancing with a young woman that catches his interest. Bradley and Lily were talking with their parents.

Thomas takes this opportunity to announce, he and Margarita would be departing in the morning. He reminds William about their early ride, and a little fishing. Bradley was watching his sisters, and the Johnson brothers. It seems as if his sisters are spending all their time with the men.

He could not put his finger on it, but a gut feeling about those two makes him uneasy. For some odd reason Bradley feels the Johnson brothers are after something.

William observes his daughters preoccupation with the young men, and wonders if he should get involved. Randall was a smooth talker. He has Monica eating out the palm of his hand. It was easy as pie, to get information out of her.

Monica was so gullible, and vain. It never occurs to her that she is supplying to much information. She is so fascinated with Randall, and his good looks. He was charming, and she never suspects the awkward questions, it was over her head.

This was a new experience for Monica. She has never met a man that could leave her at a loss for words. She takes the lead, and links her arm in his. The couple walk towards the veranda, to be alone. The man standing next to her hides a wicked smile in the darkness.

Luke is working his magic on Thelma. In his most appealing manner, he convinces her to leave the others, so they could be better acquainted. Thelma walks in the direction of the gardens and Luke follows.

She takes a seat on a nearby bench. Luke sits next to her, and begins the conversation. "Your family has done quite well for themselves haven't they?" Thelma becomes instantly suspicious. She stares into his dark eyes searching for any sign of trouble.

"I guess so." A smile plays on his lips and he continues. "Tell me more about your family." Luke was learning fast. It was obvious Thelma was not gullible and he has to put on quite a performance to deceive her. She was very keen like Bradley. He uses another tactic, and shifts the conversation.

"Why don't I just tell you how taken I'm with you." Thelma was totally off guard. The revelation surprises her. No man has ever paid such close attention to her before.

Luke was pouring it on thick, and compliments Thelma constantly. After he is confident his lies are working, he tries for a kiss. Luke was bold with his ardor. He bends his head towards Thelma, and tries to kiss her on the lips once again. She eludes the attempt the first time, but not the second time. His lips found hers, and he draws her closer on the bench.

Thelma was not expecting, the kiss to be as pleasant as it was, she was responding to his touch. The man hides his smile of satisfaction. Things are working out just fine.

Luke was holding on to Thelma and, mentions how much he needs her. The man lies to Thelma about how long he has searched to find a woman as beautiful, and loving as she.

He was very convincing, and Thelma believes every word. It has been a long time, and she longs for male attention. Luke feeds her ego. Meanwhile, Monica and Randall are discussing their future.

Randall takes the opportunity to hold Monica in his arms. The man was a master manipulator, filling her head with lies about his life and his fortune.

To seal the deal he lies about wanting a wife and family. He was saying all the things she wants to hear. The guests are leaving, and the women retire to their rooms, it has been a busy day.

Thomas, William, Bradley, and Daniel meet in the library. Bradley takes this opportunity to discuss the Johnson brothers with William. "Father what do you know about the Johnson brothers?"

William thinks for a minute before replying. "I only know that they are ranchers. They stay to themselves pretty much. Why do you ask?" Brad has a frown on his handsome face. "Oh, I don't know, it's just this strange feeling I get around them two. Maybe I am jealous, Randall was openly admiring Lily."

Thomas and William chortle at the admission. Bradley raises one brow at the men, and he join in laughing at his own insecurity. Daniel replies. "Brother, I don't think you have anything to worry about. Lily adores you."

"I know, I guess I'm over protective." Thomas responds. "Nonsense, I felt the same way about Margarita. I had to fend off a good share of admires from her mother. They are beautiful women." Bradley whole-heartedly agrees with that statement.

The next morning Thomas and William ride around the ranch. Their next stop was fishing. Bradley and Lily go into town to purchase the tickets for her parent's return to Tennessee.

They continue their ride back to the ranch. Randall and Luke are approaching. The two men wave at Bradley and Lily. Bradley stops the buggy, and greets the men. "Good morning, are you lost?" Randall rides closer to the buggy.

"No, we are going to your ranch to visit with your sisters."

Bradley's eyes narrow. The look on his face says it all. His gaze never wavers from Randall's face. "Oh, really, may I ask when did you seek approval from my father to court my sisters?"

Randall was arrogant. "I would think with them being of age. That I need no one's permission." Bradley notes the challenge, and arrogance in the man's tone. Bradley was not the type to back down.

He accepts the challenge with gusto. "Then maybe you had better ask someone, it is common practice to ask a woman's father for permission."

His light brown eyes turn hard, and his jaw muscles clench. Luke admits this was not going well, so he intervenes. "Bradley we mean no disrespect to you, or your sisters. We are on our way to ask your father for permission."

Luke does not want to ruffle Bradley's feathers. Bradley is not convinced. He replies in a cold voice. "Then let us be on our way."

Lily hears the exchange between her husband and the men. She becomes concerned. "Bradley what is the matter here?" "I'm just looking out for my sister's love that is all."

Lily places a gloved hand over his, and the ride was in silence. Bradley and Lily enter the house with the Johnson brothers in tow. William and Thomas are just coming back from there fishing trip. Margarita and Lily hug each other it was time for her parents to leave.

William and Thomas shake hands, and promise to go fishing again. Helen, Thelma, and Monica all say their goodbyes. Daniel offers to give Lily's parents a ride to the train station. Bradley and Thomas shake hands.

Bradley promise to return with Lily, and the baby. Lily mentions to Bradley. "I'm a little tired love. I'm going to lay down for a bit." Bradley turns to kiss his wife. He informs her that he would check on her soon. It was time to speak with the Johnson brothers.

Lily

William, Bradley, and the Johnson brothers go into the library to discuss the courting of his daughters. William starts the conversation. "What is this all about?" Randall steps forward, after glancing over at Bradley. "Were here sir to ask for permission to court your daughters."

William glances over at Bradley. That was the indication for Bradley to join the conversation. "It seems Thelma and Monica has taken a liking to these two gentlemen, and desires to court them." William has questions of his own. "Young man, I need to know what your intentions towards my daughters are."

Luke answers. "Sir, I assure you. Our intentions are honorable." William looks from one to the other. Then he replies. "Thelma is planning on being a Doctor do you have the means to support her? Then there is Monica, she has become accustom to comfort can you give her that?"

Randall does not like the way William is talking to them. He answers the questions with arrogance barely concealed.

"You speak to us as if we are not worthy of your daughters hand." William detects the arrogance in Randall's voice.

"I speak as a father, who only wants the best for his daughters. What do you think Brad?" Bradley glances at the two men, and his eyes lock with Randall. "I think the final decision should be left with Thelma and Monica."

William gives his permission. The men leave the room to talk with Monica and Thelma. Bradley waits for the men to leave, and then he talks with William in private. "Father, I don't trust those two. I think they want something."

William agrees. A couple of months pass, Thelma and Luke were a regular couple. She smiles more whenever he is around. It was obvious she was very smitten with Luke. Then there was Monica she and Randall were inseparable.

Bradley continues his duties with the ranch, and watching over his family. A letter arrives from Aaron and Moon

Lily

expressing their bliss exploring Europe and the honeymoon. They are enjoying their honeymoon, and would be returning in about a month. Lily was glowing with the pregnancy. She was just starting to show.

It took nothing away from her beauty. Bradley was excited about the baby. The months went by quickly. Thelma and Monica are talking marriage. Bradley did not like the ideal, but it is out of his hands.

One afternoon Lily, Thelma, and Monica decided to take a ride in the buggy to have a picnic with their men. Lily is confident that Bradley will be pleased to see her with his sisters. She takes in the surroundings and notice how far they are from the ranch.

In a nervous voice, she asks Monica, and Thelma. "Why are we so far away from the ranch?" The girls reply. "Randall and Luke told us to meet them here, and Luke assured us, he would let Brad know about the picnic." Lily has an uneasy feeling about this, but shrugs it off as tiredness.

The three women spread the blanket out under a shady tree by the river. The breeze was cool in the heat. Thelma was talking to Lily. "Are you ok? You look a little tired." "I'm fine Thelma really." Monica glances at Lily, and comments. "You look absolutely lovely Lily."

Monica's attitude toward Lily has changed after meeting Randall. There was a softer side to her. Lily replies. "Thank you Monica." The conversation ends as three riders approach the women. Lily wipes at the sweat, it must be Bradley, and the Johnson brothers.

As the riders come closer into view, Lily realizes Bradley was not among them. That was peculiar, she thinks. *Where is my husband?* Panic begins to rise in Lily. Thelma and Monica are confused. The picnic was supposed to be a family affair.

When the riders are within a few feet of the women, it was apparent the other man was not Bradley. The women are worried. What was going on? It was Randall, and Luke with another man named

Lily

Jim Clemens. The women have not seen this man before.

Randall dismounts, and so does Luke. Thelma was on her feet. "Where is Bradley?" Randall turns on Thelma, his eyes glint, and his face twist with rage. He growls in a commanding voice. "Sit down, and shut your mouth." Lily understands why she had an uneasy feeling.

The ice-cold hands of fear grips Lily, and the realization that they are in terrible danger. Thelma's eyes are wide with shock, and fear. Monica does not appreciate the way Randall is speaking to her sister. "What the hell is this Randall? Where is my brother? What is going on here?"

Luke answers her question. "I'll tell you what is going on." He marches over to Monica without uttering a single word, and slaps her hard across the face. His hands are on her shoulders shaking her like a rag doll, and blood trickles from her lip.

Lily screams! At that moment, Randall approaches Lily. The man grabs a handful of her hair, and yanks her head back so, hard that she thought her neck would snap. His free hand pulls at the bodice of her clothes shredding the front to expose her breast.

The man fixed hungry eyes upon the fullness, and he reaches out to fondle the pair. He crushes her against his chest. Lily was facing him, and smells the foulness of his breath. Randall's mouth clamps down hard on her lips.

Lily could feel his rough lips against her skin. She begins to struggle using all her might to twist her body free of his grasp. She swings her hands wildly digging her nails into his flesh. She connects with his face.

Randall curses. "You high yellow bitch, you think your better than me." He drags Lily by the arm like a sack of potatoes. Luke orders the women to get back in the buggy. Without another word, the three men guide the women away from the area. Monica and Thelma are in tears, and so was Lily.

Lily

Bradley returns from mending fences, and on his way to see Lily. He takes the stairs two at a time, and enters their room, but Lily was not there. Then he goes downstairs calling her name, and checking the rooms. Bradley runs into Daniel.

"Have you seen Lily?" Daniel replies. "I heard them saying something about a picnic." Concern enters his light brown eyes. "Come with me." Daniel follows Bradley, and they locate William.

"Father Lily, Thelma, and Monica are missing." Daniel and I are going to ride all over the ranch, if I don't return with them round up the men." His heart was racing, and he sends up a silent prayer.

"*Please God let my wife, and sisters be alright.*" William was on his feet. "I'm coming with you." The three men ride horse's looking for the three women. They search every inch of their property, but no sign of the women. At this moment, pure panic sets in on Bradley.

He orders his hands to help with the search. William sends one of his men to alert the authorities. Maybe the authorities can help look for the women. Thelma tries to comfort Monica, and Lily. The women get Monica's lip to stop bleeding, but her face was swollen, and bruised.

Thelma asks in a nervous voice. "What are we going to do?" Lily is terrified and her hands tremble. She replies. "I don't know but we are going to have to do something, they are going to kill us." Bradley, Daniel, and William ride further from the ranch.

They find carriage tracks, and three sets of horse tracks. Bradley knows that Randall and Luke have a hand in this. He makes the decision, if any harm comes to his wife or sisters; he was going to kill them. They follow the tracks until they disappear from sight. Someone swept the track away. Bradley knows the feeling of helplessness, and fear.

Lily was with child. He questions himself. *Are they all right?* Bradley

Lily

remembers the way Randall was admiring Lily, and if he laid one hand on her, he is dead. Bradley returns to the ranch and gathers more provisions, and weapons. Helen was on the porch in shock. Bradley goes over to comfort his mother.

"Mother, please contact Aaron let him know what has happen. Tell him to please stay here with you and father. I also need you to contact Thomas. Daniel and I will search for Lily."

Brad kisses his mother. "William, please stay with mother. I will find them." William knows his son was very capable.

Daniel and Bradley meet up with the other men, in the search for Lily and his sisters. The men found the blanket. Brad knells down picking up the blanket, holding it in his hands. He could still smell the scent of Lily's perfume, lingering within the blanket. Bradley looks up at the sky. He and yells out. "Lily where are you?"

Bradley keeps moving riding the horse's for hours until they are exhausted.

He only stops when the horses can go no further. Randall and Luke stop the buggy.

Both men walk around the area, and return with horses. Luke and Randall's plan is going like clockwork. The men turn and yell at the women. Luke forces the women to ride the horses. Both men are aware they can make better time by ditching the buggy. Lily notices how everything was a well laid out plan. Luke and Randall are making the women enter a cave.

There are lanterns already lit. Thelma also noticed how well organized they are. Lily whispers to Thelma.

"They had this planned all along." "You are right, but what do they want?" "I think we will find out shortly." Luke approaches the women, he was yelling at them.

"You are wondering, what is your fate? I will tell you. Bradley will pay dearly for your lives. If he doesn't then I will have no choice but to kill you." He pauses for one moment. "After we finish having our fun, isn't that right Randall?"

Randall walks over to Monica, but he was eyeing Lily. "Of course, I feel like some fun right now." He begins with Monica, and roughly pulls at her clothes. Monica tries to fend him off, but he was determined. His breath was stale, and beard rough against Monica's skin.

His hands feel dry, and chaffed, as he continues to grope her body. Monica lets out a scream! Once again, his hand meets with her face. He slaps her several more times, until she becomes limp and stiff. Randall assaults Monica in front of Thelma, and Lily. Lily and Thelma are in pure terror witnessing the assault it leaves them shaking with fear, and disgust.

Randall mounts Monica like a wild animal, and forces his way inside. His groans of sexual satisfaction fill the air, and the sound of his thrusting hips. Randall did not care about the audience.

He continues assaulting Monica, and palming her breast. Monica's body responds to his attack. Once he was finished. He climbs on top of her sweating and grunting.

Lily covers her ears to drown out the sounds and bows her head unable to stand it any longer, sobs of misery engulf her. Lily sends up a prayer. *"Dear God please send Bradley quickly."* Thelma was crying, and Luke threatens the women again. "Shut your mouth he orders." Monica was not moving. Lily whispers. "Monica, don't give up."

Thelma moves closer to Monica who was in shock from the attack. Thelma holds her sister gently rocking her back, and forth. Bradley and his men are back on the trail looking for Lily, and his sisters.

After many weeks without success, Bradley admits there is a great possibility that he would not find Lily. However, he continues the search for them. William receives a note for ransom they want fifty thousand dollars.

Lily

Aaron and Moon return as soon as possible. They make the decision to help with the search. Moon speaks to her husband. "We have to help find your sisters, and Lily." Aaron was concern for his wife's safety as well. He replies. "I will catch up to Bradley and Daniel. You stay here!"

Moon was determined. "Aaron I have lived among Indians all my life. I speak the language, and my experience as a scout will be required. You will need me to help find them." Aaron thinks on Moon's words, she was right, and he agrees.

Aaron and Moon leave to catch up with Bradley and his men. Moon manoeuvres through the harsh, rough terrain. Aaron was glad he listens to his wife. He admits he could not have found Bradley as quickly as she could. Bradley and Daniel saw riders approaching.

They have their weapon's drawn, but realize it was Aaron and Moon. Moon rushes to speak. "I had to come. You will need my help with the search for Lily, and your sisters." Aaron helps Moon dismount.

Then he replies. "We have received a ransom note for fifty thousand dollars.

William has the money ready it is in my saddlebag. They want us to make the drop in Austin Texas." Bradley digest this news he never thought they would take the women that far.

Chapter 8

He also wonders about Lily and his sisters. How are they holding up? Brad speaks.

"We have to set a trap, there is no guarantee they will not harm the women after they get the money." The group sits by the fire and put a plan together. They were already in Oklahoma. It was still a long ways to go.

Lily was exhausted from the long hours of riding. Thelma was barely holding on, and Monica did not look well at all. Randall announces they would pitch camp. They are in another cave, but this time they untie the women's hands. They allow the women to eat and drink.

Lily and Thelma overhear the men talking; it was obvious that Randall makes all the decisions. Randall continues his conversation with Luke and Jim. "I am sure William has received the ransom note, and pretty sure he wants his precious daughters alive. He will pay, and we will be very rich men." Jim Clemens did not like the arrangement. He replies. "I never agreed to harm the women."

Randall was harsh. "Don't you go getting yourself a conscience now? If we are caught, you will hang just like me, and Luke." Luke pauses then replies. "That Lily is a hellcat. I can't wait to have my fun with her." Lily trembles with fear they are going to rape each one of them.

Bradley and his men have arrived in Austin. After weeks of hard riding, Bradley makes the drop. They move out of sight so they can see who will make the pickup. It was hard, but they wait.

The sun was just going down. There was a stocky man coming towards the money. He looks around to make sure no one was there, and then picks up the saddlebags.

As soon as the man was about to leave Bradley comes out of hiding with a pistol in his hand. He steps out in the open, and calls to the man. The man looks up, and faces Bradley. He tries to run but Aaron and Daniel are blocking his escape. Bradley's voice was cold, and it holds death. "Don't you move? Or I will blow your head off!"

Bradley walks up to the man, and removes the saddlebags from his grasp. Jim Clemens fears for his life. He has no doubt that Bradley means ever word. Bradley wants answers. "Where is my wife, and sisters?" Jim Clemens has a blank stare on his face. He was shaking all over.

Jim has heard stories about Bradley Thomas, and he was fool enough to cross him. Jim Clemens finds his voice. "I don't know what you are talking about." Bradley furrows his brow, and his eyes narrow. His voice was cold, and without emotion. "Let me see if I can jog your memory."

He puts the pistol against the man's head, and cocks the hammer back. Suddenly the man speaks. "I will take you to them. It was not my ideal. It was Randall and Luke." The anger inside of Bradley was at full peak. He wants to squeeze the trigger.

However, he needs the man alive to find the women.

Bradley ties Jim Clemens hands, and begins asking questions. Bradley asks in a hard voice. "Has any one harmed my family?" Jim's eyes fill with fear, but he finds his voice. "Randall and Luke have already raped your sister. As far as I know, they have not touched your wife yet."

Bradley was enraged. He knows they have very little time to reach the women, before more harm befalls them. Moon holds on to Aaron, she was crying. Aaron tries to calm her down. "Moon we will find them they will be ok."

Moon looks at Aaron, and replies. "They have already raped one of them. This is horrible. We must hurry." Bradley and his group mount their horses. It was a race with time to save the women.

Meanwhile, in the cave Randall and Luke pace, they are waiting on Jim Clemens to return with the money. He should be arriving shortly. Luke decides he wants his turn with Lily, and Randall looks at Monica in disgust.

He settles for Thelma. She would do just fine. The two men approach the women. Monica is listless and matted blood covers her face. She was still in shock from the assault by Randall.

Randall was dragging Thelma to her feet. Thelma's voice was shrill. "Take your hands off of me! My brothers will kill you for this!" Randall shoves Thelma to the ground. He was ripping off her clothes, and his greedy eyes admire every inch of her.

Thelma screams and fights, to no avail. Randall was pulling her hair, and bruising her lips with his. His hands were all over her. He paid no attention to her cries. Monica quietly struggles to her feet after hearing her sister's screams. She picks up a rock, and lunges toward Randall.

Randall hears Monica and he moves in time, with his pistol in his hand. He turns and swings the butt of his pistol and it slams against Monica's temple. There was a terrible noise, and she falls to the ground bleeding.

Luke was trying to attack Lily, but she was clawing at his face. Her nails dig into his flesh. Luke lifts his hand, and strikes her full force in the face. He was too strong for her, but she continues to fight. Luke was on top of Lily, and she screams.

The next thing she knows. The weight of Luke is off her. When she opens her eyes, Bradley was standing over her. Aaron and Daniel are pulling Randall off Thelma. Randall and Aaron begin fist fighting. Aaron sends a bone crushing blows to Randall's face. The cave fills with the sound of bones being broken from the force.

Randall folds, and falls to the ground. Luke was quick to get on his feet, and charges Bradley. The two men tussle on the ground. Luke's face twists with rage, and he pulls a knife. The man clutches the weapon, and dives on top of Bradley, trying to stab him with the knife.

Lily

Bradley was too powerful for Luke; he knocks the other man off him with little effort. Luke makes a second attempt to get to his feet. Once again, he lunges at Bradley with the knife. This time Bradley draws his pistol, and squeezes the trigger. There was a loud echoing noise, and the bullet hits Luke in the shoulder.

Luke falls to the ground with a thud. Daniel ties Randall and Luke's hands. Aaron was dragging them to their feet. Daniel and Bradley cover the women. Bradley knells over Monica. He lifts her head. She was hurt bad, and her eyes roll around in her head.

She tries to speak. "You are here! Thank God. Is Thelma safe?" Bradley was holding back tears. He knows his sister was not going to make it. He replies. "Thelma is safe." Monica smiles, her eyes close and then she was gone. Moon, Thelma, and Lily all hug each other. The women sobs are bitter for the loss of Monica.

Aaron and Daniel both hold back the tears. They have to be strong for the women. Daniel asks Bradley. "How are we going to tell mother and William?" Bradley hugs his brothers. Then he replies. "I don't know." They all decide to bury Monica in Texas.

They had no other choice. Lily clings to Bradley for dear life. "I'm, so very sorry. I'm so afraid." Bradley draws Lily to his chest. "It is not your fault. It is the Johnson brothers. I promise on my sister's grave. She will have retribution." His eyes become hard, and cold. Bradley has never been more angry, or remorseful in his life.

In his mind anger and hatred rages toward the men who caused his family grief. Aaron approaches Bradley "Come on Bradley the men are taking the Johnson brothers, and Jim Clemens back to stand trial. Let's take the women back home."

Bradley nods in agreement. "Give me a moment to say good bye to Monica." They all said their good byes. The ride back to St. Louis was long and tiring. Bradley was concern for the women so they rest more often. He was especially worried for Lily she was so close to giving birth.

He did not want to jeopardize her, and the baby. The closer they get to the ranch the more Bradley dreads. He would have to break the news to his folks. Helen, William, Thomas, and Margarita were on the veranda when Bradley and the rest ride up.

Helen scans their faces. She did not see Monica. "Where is your sister?" Aaron replies before Bradley. "Mother, father, please let's go in the house not out here." Margarita runs over to Lily she was alive, but her clothes were torn and her face was dirty, and swollen. It looks like a bruise on her cheek.

Margarita hugs her daughter close, and walks in the library with the rest of the family. William feels something terrible has happen. Why else would Monica not be here. William holds Helen as if bracing her for the news. Bradley's light eyes are cloudy.

He looks at both of his parents, and gently tells them that Monica is dead. Helen's voice was shrill "No, no, no. It cannot be. Bradley please tell me this is not so." Tears are in her eyes. She clutches at her heart. Bradley places an arm on her shoulders, and guides her to a sofa.

He glances at Helen's face, which twists in pain. "Mother she is gone. I 'am sorry." William immediately leaves the room. He returns with a shotgun clutched in his hand. Thomas knows William was ready to kill the boys responsible for his daughter's death.

Thomas gently speaks to William. "My friend, you are hurt and angry. I would feel the same if it was my daughter. However this will not bring her back." William looks at Thomas. He admits he was right.

William hands the gun to Thomas, and breaks down in front of him. "I have lost my baby Thomas. Those rotten bastards will pay." Bradley was thankful that Thomas, and Margarita were here. Thelma knells down beside her mother.

"Monica died trying to protect me from Randall. Thelma chokes back tears. "He raped her in front of us. Lily and I were next on his list."

Tears fall down her face each time she thinks of what happen. "I feel so violated." Helen hugs her daughter close and let unrestrained tears flow. Moon and Lily join the family in there time of sorrow.

It was clear to Lily that her husband was hurting even though he remains strong on the outside. A week after Monica's death the family has a memorial service for her. Now maybe they could try to get on with their lives. Thomas and Margarita leave after the service.

Lily promises her parents she would stay safe. Bradley watches over his wife and sister. Thelma was still withdrawn, but she slowly was recovering from their episode. A trial date was set for the Johnson brothers, and Jim Clemens.

All three men are charged with murder, and kidnapping. The sentence was to hang all three men. Bradley could move on with his family. The baby was due any day now. Moon keeps Lily entertained, and Thelma would join in.

Helen stays close to Thelma after all she was the last of her daughters. William was dealing with the loss as best he could. Daniel was taking part in the business, and so was Aaron. Brad figures they are stepping up to the plate. Aaron was trying to show Bradley he could handle the business, and he and Lily could start a life of their own.

Aaron was speaking with Bradley on that very subject. "I know time is getting near for the baby to be born. You and Lily will be leaving in about six months. I thought we could take a load off your mind by proving to you. Daniel and I can handle everything."

Bradley shakes his brother's hand. "Thank you Aaron. I really appreciate what

you two are doing." Daniel walks up.
Bradley slaps him on the shoulder, and hugs
him close.

"I know you and I have had our
differences Daniel, but you're my younger
brother, and I love you." Daniel looks at his
brother. "Are you getting soft on me Brad?"
Bradley smiles at Daniel, and Aaron. The
three men walk towards the house. Lily and
Moon were sitting on the porch.

Aaron leans over to his wife, and
places a soft kiss on her cheek. Moon smiles
up at her husband. "What is that for?" Aaron
returns the smile. "Just because I love you,
and I'm the luckiest man in the world."
Bradley joins Lily, and compliments his
wife.

He whispers in her ear. "My love,
thank you for being there for me. You have
been there through the bad as well as the
good. I love you." Bradley kisses his wife on
her cheek. She was as beautiful as ever.
Even with child, she was dazzling.

Everyone agrees it was chilly out tonight. They decide to retire in the house. Brad notices Lily stumble trying to get out of the chair. He was at her side "Is everything alright love." Lily tries to be braver than she was feeling.

"The baby is coming. My water has broken, and I am having terrible pains! Bradley, please, I need a doctor." He picks Lily up, and starts up the stairs. He was excited and apprehensive at the same time. He places Lily on the bed.

Moon was right behind him. She instructs him to get Doctor Burns. Aaron let the rest of the family know that the baby was coming. Bradley has waited for this day for nine months. Now that it was upon him, he was a nervous wreck.

He tries to stay with Lily, but his mother, Moon, and Thelma kick him out. Helen tells him to wait with the men, and everything would be fine. Brad paces back and forth. Each time Lily screams he almost jumps out of this skin.

Lily

Daniel and Aaron where trying to calm Brad down. They decide that a stiff drink was in order. William gingerly agrees. William was reminiscing about the time his children were born. "I remember how it was each time your mother went into labor to have you children.

"I thought I was going to have a heart attack." Brad knows his father is looking forward to the baby being born. Bradley was replying to his father's comment. "William, what if something goes wrong? Lily is screaming an awful lot. I hope she is all right. I'm going to check on her."

"Now hold on son, you're not going to get in that room. Just try and calm down everything will be fine." William notes Bradley was worried, and this is his first child. Lily was in a lot of pain, and she feels like something is wrong. The women are still mopping her brow.

Doctor Burns arrives. The Doctor has a concern look on his face! He beckons to Helen. "I'm afraid that Lily might not be

able, or strong enough to have this child."
Helen was concern. "What is it?" "The
child is large. She is a small frame woman,
and she is fully dilated."

Lily lets out a blood-curling scream.
Doc Burns instructs her to push. When that
did not work, he makes the incision to widen
the canal. It would help Lily birth the child.
Lily was exhausted. All she remembers was
a cry then she was out.

She wakes from the smelling salt.
She was wide-awake now. "Where is my
baby?" Fear grips Lily. Doc burns has a
serious look on his face. Her fears begin
gnawing at her. She says a silent prayer.
"Oh God let the baby be alright." Helen
comes towards Lily with a bundle.

She places the small bundle in
Lily's arms. It was her son, and he was
asleep. Bradley enters the room after
speaking with Doc Burns. He walks over to
his wife. His light eyes glisten with tears.

Lily panics. "Bradley what is the
matter?" "Nothing Love, what are we going

to name our son?" Bradley was smiling down at Lily.

"I like Bradley Theodore Thomas." "I love it! That will suit this young man. For short let's call him BT." BT was beginning to make his presence known. He was crying. Lily coos the baby, and he quiets down. Her heart was full with love and happiness. This was their first child, and he was a precious gift.

All of the family members join them in the blessed occasion of BT's birth. The family decides to take turns with the baby, so Lily could regain her strength. Lily notices that Bradley was happy about BT, but a look of concern still lingers on his handsome face.

Lily waits until they are alone to ask the question. "Bradley, love what is troubling you?" Bradley raises one brow at his wife. He was off guard. "It's nothing that we need to discuss right now my love. We can discuss it later, after you recover from giving birth."

Lily was not going to let him off the hook so easy. "No, Bradley! I want to discuss it now please. I'm alright." Brad knows that look. There was determination in those grey eyes. "Ok love. What I need to tell you will have no bearing on the way I feel about you. I love you just the same."

Lily was taking in every word. "What is it Bradley?" "I spoke with Doc. Burns. He thinks the possibility of you having more children is slim in chance. You went through a rough time with BT." Lily digests this information. Her eyes are misty.

"I will never be able to give you more children?" Lily hears her voice become shrill. Bradley sits on the bed, and hugs Lily close. He whispers in her ear.

"Not to worry Lily, I love you! You have given me a son. That is enough for me. I thank God above for you blessing my life. You have brought so much happiness, and Lily, that is enough for me."

Lily listens to her husband's words. If Bradley was willing to accept, the possibility of no more children then so would she. She would still have Bradley and BT in her life, and that would be enough for her. Day's turn into weeks, Lily fully recovers from the birth of their son. She absolutely enjoys her son. He was beautiful. BT has smooth wavy hair, and his eyes are grey. He is a handsome boy, just like his father.

When BT gets older, he would break many hearts. Bradley was walking towards the house with the mail in his hand. He enters the room where Lily is sitting, and asks Thelma to take BT. It was time to have a talk with Lily in private. Lily releases her son to Thelma.

She gives her full attention to her husband. "What is it Bradley?" "I have received a letter from Thomas, and your mother. They will be here in a week's time. They want to see their grandson, and of course us. Thomas tells me that the house is nearly complete.

We should be moving in five months." Lily thinks the information over.

Then she asks her questions. "Is this what you want Bradley? My place is with you. I know that you originally decided to move to Tennessee to keep me close to my parents. We have lived here for so long with your family. I will understand if you change your mind."

Bradley raises a quizzical brow at his wife. "I have not changed my mind love. I have asks you too many times to wait. You have put this on hold more times, than I care to count. I am a man of his word. We will be moving in five months!"

Lily smiles up at her husband. "Bradley Thomas, I love you, and thank you darling." He reaches out, and enfolds her into his embrace. It has been weeks since he has made passionate love to her. Bradley was overdue.

Bradley whispers into Lily's ear. "Come with me up stairs. I need you so badly." She hears the urgency in his voice. Bradley picks Lily up into his strong arms, and climbs the stairs two at a time. In their room Bradley place light kisses on her neck, and shoulders. He expertly removes her clothing.

Chapter 9

She helps remove his pants, and shirt. Strong hands move over Lily's body. His tongue was inside her mouth, like a man dying from thirst. Her hands twist in his hair, and then she slides both hands down his back. She slips her tongue inside his ear.

She moves on towards his neck. Her mouth makes contact with nipples on his strong broad chest, and she touches the hairs on his chest. They are both at a fevered pitch. The two of them are breathing hard, and uneven.

His mind explodes from Lily touching, and caressing his body. He has taught Lily how to pleasure a man, and she was good at it.

Bradley draws Lily on top of him. She slides soft legs to straddle him, and feels his hard manhood at full peak. It was hard

for him to control his need, and he was
about to explode. Lily moves her body
expertly over his manhood. She begins to
move back, and forth.

She feels the warmth of his manhood
between her thighs. Lily was at an all-time
high with the lovemaking. Bradley moans
in a hoarse voice with pleasure. He has
never hungered sexually for any one woman
in his life. However, this was his Lily, and
she was not like other women.

Lily was moaning, and calling
Bradley's name. How she loved this man.
Only he possesses her very soul. Afterwards
they are exhausted, but very satisfied with
each other.

A couple of hours later Bradley and
Lily are enter the dining area. His parents
approach the two of them. Helen was very
pleased with the birth of her grandson. She
was giddy, and smiling at the couple. "I
must tell the two of you. How much we
love our grandson. His birth has brought so
much happiness into our lives."

Bradley realizes his mother was thinking of Monica. William was commenting. "You know son, the birth of our grandson has made a wonderful addition to the family. We will miss him when the two of you move." Bradley realizes the conversation with his parents would not be easy.

He was determined to remind them of their plans. Bradley waits until dinner was over. He uses this moment to mention his plans. "Mother, William, I feel this is a good time, to let the family know that Lily and I will be moving to Tennessee in five months.

You are more than welcome to come to visit, and likewise we will bring your grandson to visit the both of you."

Helen looks to William as if she needs his strength. William answers calmly. "Son we are not senile. We know that you are moving with your family. You are a man. You have to make your way in this world. I have given you all you need son."

Lily

Bradley walks over and shakes his father's hand. He leans over to kiss his mother. Brad feels as if a large weight lifts off his shoulders. Aaron and Moon are listening to the conversation, and Daniel has a date. Thelma has taken a liking to BT.

Aaron was talking to Bradley. "I have taken the liberty of employing a couple more men to help with the cattle drives. The books are up to date. I know Daniel and I will be able to manage. Brad I would be honored if you would take a look at some paper work."

Brad really admires Aaron's dedication running the business. Daniel has the business down pretty well. He was still in training. Nevertheless, he was coming along. Bradley was questioning Aaron about Daniel's mystery woman.

"Who is this young woman? She keeps my younger brother away from the dinner table at least three nights of the week?" Aaron smiles at Brad. "I believe her name is Emily, and she comes from a respectable family." Bradley gives Aaron a knowing eye. He knows this conversation ends in front of the women.

Thelma shocks the family with her announcement. She was going to move to Europe, in a couple of weeks. Bradley's gaze settles on his sister with concern. "Thelma you sure you want to do this? You don't have to prove anything to us."

Thelma thinks before replying. "You are right big brother. I do not, but I need to get on with my life. Europe has excellent schools of medicine." Helen was worried she asks. "Thelma dear, I know you are still hurting over the loss of Monica. Please do not be hasty."

Thelma inhales deeply, then she responds with strength that surprises her. "Mother it is time for me to move forward. Monica gave her life for me. I know she would want me to go on with my life."

That was the end of that conversation. Thelma was moving to Europe. After dinner, the family sits around holding BT. He was the highlight of the evening. Daniel returns in time to accompany the men in the library for cigars, and brandy. Bradley takes this opportunity to question his brother about his mystery woman.

"So, Daniel who is this fair maiden that has your undivided attention of late." Daniel looks Bradley square in the eyes, and replies. "Her name is Emily Steward. I want to tell you all about her, but there are some complicated circumstances involved."

Aaron joins the conversation. "Go on Daniel, this should be interesting. I can hardly wait. Do tell." Daniel looks as if he is a caged animal. "Well she is a wonderful woman. She is in love with me not my family fortune. We like the same things, and we have a lot in common."

Bradley detects something amiss with this woman. "So Daniel what is the big secret?" Daniel lowers his eyes and replies. "She is a white woman. That is why I keep the relationship a secret." William almost falls out of his chair.

He was furious. "Have you lost your natural mind Daniel?" Do you know the price a black man will pay if he is caught with a white woman?"

Aaron and Bradley are both in shock. Bradley finds his voice. "Daniel, please tell me that you are kidding." Daniel was firm. "I assure you all that Emily and I are in love. What is the color of our skin to do with it?" William explodes! "I will tell you what it has to do with it. My father was a sharecropper on a plantation, and he fell for a white woman.

They hung him from the highest tree. I would not want that to befall my son." Daniel was furious! "I'm a grown man father you cannot dictate my life. I have to make my own mistakes."

Bradley and Aaron try to intervene. "Daniel, please think about what this can cause! Is it really worth it? You are jeopardizing the safety of our family."

Daniel would hear no more from any of them, and storms out of the room.

Lily

The three men stare after him. William sits in his chair with a worried look on his face. Bradley and Aaron remember the childhood stories about their grandfather to well.

Daniel continues to see Emily. She was the best thing that has ever happen to him. He loves her. Emily was pale, with sea green eyes, and long chestnut brown hair. She was well proportioned, and Daniel could not get enough of her.

They have been lovers now for some time. It was hard to be careful all the time, but so far, no one knows except Daniels family. He has faith that they will never betray him. Emily makes Daniel feel like a complete man. Out of all the women, Daniel has known they never made him feel the way she did.

Emily was breathless, and her hair flows about the shoulders. She has been riding for a while, and finally reaches their secret meeting place. It was a secluded area, and their private love nest. Emily has lost count of how many times they made love. She quietly waits in the darkness for Daniel.

Emily hears a noise, the sound of footsteps. A tall figure exits the shadows, and she instantly recognizes Daniel. She would know Daniels body anywhere; she quickly rises and enters his embrace. "Hello sweetheart I have missed you terribly."

Daniel could not get enough of her. He encircles her waist drawing her body up against his chest. The need was urgent, and he wants Emily right now, not able to contain his hunger much longer.

He touches her silky long hair, and gently lowers her clothing. Daniel lowers his hands to touch and massage her sweet soft skin. The scent of lavender intoxicates his senses.

Emily moans, and revels in his touch. She feels like putty in his hands. Emily draws his mouth closer slipping her tongue inside tasting the deliciousness of his mouth. She follows a path with her tongue over his lean sinewy body. Daniel's long fingers circle then invade the core of her private area. Long fingers gently move within her, making her gasp with pleasure.

Lily

She was on fire with lust no other man has ever made her feel this way. Emily brushes her lips against Daniel's nipples, the motion causes him to become taut and erect with need.

Daniel pulls her farther down, grasping her hips, spreading her legs wider, and lowers his mouth to her cave of pleasure. He was inhaling the sweet scent of her juices flowing. He engages his tongue tasting all of her; it was unlike anything he has ever known. Emily draws his head down further twisting her fingers in his hair, and calling out his name.

Daniel changes the position placing his weight on top of her. The look of bliss on her face captures him and he becomes more erect from the moans of pleasure. She slides from underneath Daniel forcing him backward. Once positioned, she joins him placing her body on top. Her tongue slides smoothly across his nipples, stomach, and down past his navel.

Daniel convulses from the warmth of her tongue against his genitals. Her mouth covers the long hard shaft in a rhythmic motion lingering with purpose. His sense where heighten by their lovemaking, the blood rushes to his head.

Daniel was on fire responding to her every touch. He surrenders as her fingers rest on his manhood. Emily gives herself to him wholeheartedly.

It was a never-ending feeling of desire that shakes them both. He could not hold back much longer. His body was out of control with desire, and making love to her was indescribable.

He shifts his weight, on top of Emily, guiding himself inside her warmth. She closes her eyes waiting to feel his large shaft. The sounds of pleasure escape her lips, as he thrust his hips in and out, up and down. Emily clings to Daniel as if he was a life raft.

When it was over, she cuddles in his arms on the soft grass. Daniel waits a couple of minutes before he replies. "I told my family about you Emily. They are worried about my safety, and not happy with the situation."

Emily listens carefully to Daniel's words then she responds. "Daniel, I love you with all my heart. Please do not tell me that you do not want me anymore. I could not survive without you."

Daniel turns to look into Emily's green eyes, and admits no matter what the cost, he could not leave Emily behind.

"Emily love! I to feel the same, but it will not change the situation. My life is in danger and so is yours." Emily thinks for a few minutes and grins at Daniel as a solution comes to mind. Her eyes twinkle. "What if we move to Europe, no one would object to us being together?"

Daniel thinks on Emily's words. "You might have a solution to our predicament." Daniel was now thinking. "We could catch a boat not at the same time of course, but the same destination, then we could be together."

Emily offers monetary support for their quest. She was looking forward to a life with Daniel. The more she thinks about sharing her life with Daniel the better it sounds. She has no problem leaving her present life behind. At least they would be together.

Daniel has enough money put to the side to purchase a home in Europe. This would be perfect. The couple formulate a plan of action. It was their life and nothing could stop them from being together.

William looks weary and tired. Aaron walks over to his father. "Father, I know you are worried about Daniel. However all we can do is hope that he comes to his senses." Bradley was in his own thoughts about his younger brother's decision.

Even though he did not like the risk, he was taking. He would support him. Bradley offers his advice. "William stay calm this storm will pass and Daniel will figure this out give him time. If he doesn't then all we can do is lend our support."

Lily

William nods in agreement. Lily wakes to the sound of BT crying, and she was by his side immediately. BT smiles at his mother. Bradley was in the doorway, watching Lily bath their son, and change his diaper.

She was singing to BT, and he quiets down. She holds him in her arms and walks over to the rocking chair to breast-feed. Bradley makes his presence known to Lily.

She was a bit startled. "Good morning love." Lily's eyes are shinning with happiness, and contentment. Bradley pulls up a chair to sit with Lily, and watch her feed BT. "He is getting so big Bradley." "Yes he is love. He will be a young man before you know it." Lily is curious. She wonders what is on Bradley's mind.

It was normal for him to help with BT, but today was somehow different. She has lived with him long enough to know when something was troubling him.

"Bradley is everything alright?"
Bradley scans his wife's face. "The family is
worried about Daniel. He is seeing a young
white woman named Emily. We are afraid
for his safety, and ours."

Lily listens to what Bradley has to
say. Then she replies. "Bradley is it fair to
judge Emily by the color of her skin? I know
first-hand how it feels. It makes no
difference if a person is one race or another.
We cannot help who we fall in love with."

Bradley listens to his wife's words,
and admits she was right. "Lily what do you
suggest that I do?" she thinks on the
question before she answers. "Help him any
way you can." Bradley rises to his feet. He
walks over to Lily, and places a kiss on her
forehead.

"What would I do without you?"
Lily just smiles at Bradley. She was still
smiling when he leaves the room.

Bradley catches up with Aaron. He
was going to discuss the situation about
Daniel. "Aaron where is father?" "He's at

breakfast with mother, and Thelma." "We need to speak with them." Aaron follows Brad to the breakfast area. Moon enters the room saying her good mornings.

Bradley greets his family, and starts the conversation. "William and mother I have thought over Daniels plight. I know we have to sit down, and figure out a way to help him with this matter." William looks sharply at Bradley.

He replies. "I have discussed this matter with your mother. We are in agreement that this could turn into an ugly situation."

Aaron joins the conversation. "Daniel has to decide what he wants to do. If he is determined to be with this woman there is nothing we can do but support him."

William cuts in. "At what cost? Are you telling me it is more important to jeopardize his life? We are talking about a woman." Daniel was entering the room he overhears the conversation, and responds to the remark. "None of you have to worry about me bringing any danger to our family or myself.

Emily and I have decided to move to Europe. Color doesn't seem to matter there." Bradley brows draw together. "What of the business? Have you taken anyone other than yourself in consideration? How are you to elope with Emily without being discovered?"

Daniel does not want to feud with Bradley about this. Bradley notes the pain in his brother's eyes. He rephrases his questions. "Daniel I know you are in love with this woman. You are willing to give up everything for her. Are you prepared to let go of the people who love you the most? I will help you, even though I don't totally agree with your methods."

Daniel breathes a sigh of relief. Aaron lends his support. Now the three brothers are looking at William. He looks at his sons, and admits defeat. William chuckles, at least his sons stick together.

"What the hell. I have done worst things. Daniel as your father I will help you get to Europe as safe as possible. We are going to have to use the cover of darkness. I can pay for your passage on a ship."

Daniel hugs his father. "Thank you all for helping me. I truly love this woman." Helen waves her son closer." Daniel you are my youngest son. I love you dearly. I only want you to be happy."

"I know mother, and thank you." Thelma and Moon hug Daniel. The women wish him well. The three men sit down to put a plan into action. The plan was for Aaron to pay for passage on the boat for Thelma, Emily, and Daniel. In the meantime Bradley and Daniel are leaving to meet Emily at their secrete place.

Soon after Emily arrives, Daniel explains the plan to Emily. All she has to do is slip out the house, and they would be waiting to transport her to the ship. Since Thelma was leaving for Europe also, they would use Thelma as Emily's Maid. This would help both women achieve their goal.

No one would bother them if Emily travels with a companion. Thelma was not keen on the idea, but she loves her brother. She goes along with the plan. The next evening Emily meets Daniel at their secret place for the last time.

She was anxious, to be with him. Daniel hugs her and whispers. "Be careful, my love soon we will have a life together." Daniel places the ticket in her hand. All Emily has to do is sneak out at midnight.

Bradley and Aaron would be waiting with Daniel. Once Emily arrives, they would take the women to the ship. Daniel would board shortly after.

Emily returns home. Ralph Stewart, Emily's, father was a very powerful man. He was wealthy, privileged, and one of St. Louis socialites. Ralph was a man to fear, and has connections all over the city. Emily looks across the table at both her parents. She was happy this would be her last evening with them.

Lily

Emily wishes she could discuss Daniel with them, but she knows her father would not hear of her with a black man.

It does not matter that he has Indian heritage, all he would see is the color of his skin. Marge Stewart was frail and kind hearted, but she was a bell of the south and whites did not mix with the blacks.

Emily did not care what they think she never thought of people that way. All she knows is she loves Daniel Thomas, and wants to be his wife at any cost. Emily hides a couple of travelling bags outside. She takes only what she needs ready for midnight.

Aaron and Bradley are in position. Emily manages to leave her house everyone was asleep. She collects her belongings, and rides to meet Daniel at their secret place.

Daniel was just arriving. Emily runs into his arms. "I'm ready love." Daniel holds her against his chest, and lifts her face to look her in the eyes.

"Emily, you sure you want to do this?" Emily saw the anticipation in Daniel's face. "I will go where ever I have to, even to the end of the earth to be with you." It was settle Daniel helps Emily into the waiting buggy. The men load Emily's things on the buggy.

Once they were satisfied, they drive into the night. Daniel would meet up with them an hour or two later by horse. Emily and Thelma ride together in the buggy, and both women are nervous about their destination. William paid a pretty penny for their passage at this time of night. The two women look at each other from head to toe.

Chapter 10

Emily speaks first. "Hello Thelma. I 'am sorry we had to meet like this, but have no doubt I love your brother with all my heart." Thelma decides Emily was a good person, and she likes her.

Emily must be in love with Daniel. Why else would she take such a chance? The two women chat along the way when their destination was in view Thelma gracefully pretends to be in Emily's service.

All goes well. Daniel arrives as promised he pays his passage, and boards the ship. He breathes a sigh of relief. All he has to do is keep his distance until they get to Europe. Bradley breathes a sigh of relief and sends up a silent prayer. *"God be with our siblings."*

Aaron replies. "They will be fine! At least we know Daniel and Thelma will be safe." Brad nods in agreement. The men return home. Lily was waiting for Bradley's return. "How did it go? Are they safe?" Brad responds. "Yes love. They all boarded safely."

Brad put his hand on Lily's waist, and walks deeper into the house. He goes to let his father know that Daniel and Thelma have boarded the ship. Moon and Aaron are bringing Helen up to speed.

The days pass, Thomas and Margarita have arrived. They could not wait to see BT, and the rest of the family. William was delighted that Thomas, and Margarita have returned. Helen hugs Margarita. The women became great friends.

They both shared in the joy of their grandson. Lily hugs her mother, and then Thomas. Bradley has a strong handshake for his father-in-law. He was speaking with Thomas. "Did you have a good trip?" "Not bad. Your house is just about complete. I know you will be very pleased with the result."

Lily

Brad's light brown eyes meet grey. "I have all the faith in the world in you Thomas." The two men walk to the library, to join the others. Thomas was asking about Daniel. Brad explains in his smooth voice, and brings Thomas up to speed.

Thomas finally gets to hold his grandson after wresting him away from the women. Thomas notes his grey eyes. He was cute as a button. He expresses to Bradley how proud he was. It was time for dinner, and everyone gathers at the dinner table.

Each telling his or her story for the evening, Helen instructs the help make a special meal for Margarita and Thomas. The menu consists of baked ham, glazed sweat potatoes, a young turkey with dressing, and all the trimmings.

Margarita compliments Helen on her choice of menu. After dinner, the women sit in the parlour. The men leave to conduct business in the library. William and Thomas were laughing about their grandson. The Maid brings in coffee, and brandy, and the men sit down to discuss current events.

William starts the conversation. "Well, Thomas, will we get to do some more fishing?" Thomas grey eyes light up. "Well of course. I was hoping you would ask." Bradley and Aaron watch the two men acting like schoolchildren.

Bradley interrupts their laughter. "Father, Thomas has told me that the house in Tennessee is almost complete. I would like to talk with you about the division of the herds."

Aaron pays close attention. So does William. William pauses as if choosing his words carefully. "Bradley I have considered this and I have come up with an amount that you will fine fair. One hundred fifty head of cattle."

Bradley notes the amount. Then he answers. "I feel that is very fair." Aaron joins the conversation. "Brad have you decided how many hands you will need to set up in Tennessee?"

"Thomas is helping with the hiring of the men. I would like to ask you Thomas, if you would be willing to be in charge when Lily and I travel back, and forth to visit my parents."

Thomas considers Brads offer. Then he replies. "Only when you're away, I think I can do that." Brad was pleased. "Good then it's settled." William and Thomas continued their conversation. Aaron and Brad discuss the loose ends of his departing.

The next morning Bradley meets Aaron in the breakfast area the two men greet each other. Aaron was asking Brad about joining him for a ride. "Sure I will join you Aaron. I want to make sure everything will run smooth before I leave."

Moon and Lily join the men. Bradley was asking the women to join them for an early morning ride.

Aaron holds the chair for Moon. Bradley walks over and kisses his wife on the cheek. "It's been a long time since you have taken a ride with me love." His light brown eyes twinkle with mischief. He knows each time they ride together they stop to make love.

Lily lets a smile touch her lips. She replies. "I would love to go for a ride. Mother has BT all afternoon." Moon and Lily put on their riding clothes, and join the men. Moon was speaking to Lily. "I love riding, you feel so free with the wind behind your back."

Aaron rides alongside his wife. Moon and Aaron are so similar they are perfect for one another. They both share so much in common. Lily replies. "I agree it's like no freedom I have ever known." Bradley begins to chuckle. "Is that right?" His handsome face was glowing with mischief today.

Brad and Aaron dismount, then help the women. Lily looks at the huge amount of land before them. Bradley discusses his business with Aaron, and they return to the women. Brad stands behind Lily encircling her into his strong arms.

Lily

Lily speaks first. "I have grown to love it here Bradley." Brad hears the emotion in Lily's words. "Are you having second thoughts about the move Lily?" She turns to face her husband.

"No, I just will miss all of your family. I was an only child, and never had the closeness that you and your family have."

Brad replies. "You will have the best of both worlds love." She smiles up at her husband. Shortly after the couples mount their horses, and ride for a while. Later they returned to the house. The baby was crying and fussy when they return. He wants his mother. It makes Lily proud when she holds her son, and he quiets down.

William receives a letter from Thelma and Daniel. Thelma speaks of the beauty of England. She has found her place in the world. According to her letter, Daniel and Emily were married they have settled in a very nice home.

Emily asks Thelma to stay with them. Thelma accepts. They want everyone to know that they were safe. They all send their love. William reads the letter to the family. This was a great relief for Helen.

Bradley and Aaron also breathed a sigh of relief. Thomas wants to spend a little time with his daughter. Together they walk to the veranda. "Lily we are looking forward to your return." She thinks for a moment. "That is funny, I just mention to Bradley how accustom I have become to being around his family."

It was Thomas turn to weigh his words carefully. "Lily, I know when you first left you were a young girl. You have become a wife, and mother in a short amount of time."

Thomas has a worried look on his face. Lily hears the strain in his voice. She stops to face her father because something was troubling him.

Lily

Lily gently probes. "Father is everything all right?" "Lily I don't want to put any burdens upon you. It is your mother." Lily eyes are wide now with concern.

"What is wrong with Mother?" Thomas was upset! "It's her heart Lily. Margarita had a mild heart attack a couple months back. She would not let me tell you."

Lily's eyes are cloudy. "Has she been to a Doctor? Thomas runs his fingers through his wavy hair in frustration. "Yes! They do not have much knowledge about the heart. Doc. told me to keep your mother as calm as possible. All these years, I have struggled to provide for my family. Your mother has always been by my side through it all."

Lily walks over to her father, and hugs him. "It's going to be alright! I will be there to help you with mother." Thomas smiles at his daughter. "I just feel so helpless. I don't know what I would do without your mother."

Lily knows this was true. They walk back in the house to join the rest of the family. Lily has already made her mind up. She would discuss this in private with her husband. Bradley was holding BT. He scans his wife's face, and she looks upset.

Bradley hands BT to his mother, and quickly walks over to Lily. "Is everything alright, Lily?" She looks into Bradley's concerned eyes. "I need to speak with you in private please." Bradley excuses them both.

Once they reach the library Bradley wants to find out what is bothering Lily. "Okay Love, what is the matter?" Lily turns to face Bradley. "My father just informed me that my mother had a mild heart attack a couple of months ago. She would not let father tell me."

Bradley has a concern look on his face. His mind was racing. How could he deny Lily anything, after all the times she stood by him? After a few moments, Bradley replies. "What do you want to do? If you would like to move now we can." A frown crosses her brow.

Lily

"I know, but BT is still so young. I have to be there for my parents. Yes darling I want to leave now, my mother needs me."

Bradley walks closer to his wife, and puts a comforting arm on her shoulder. Then he replies. "Then it is settled, we shall be leaving in a couple of weeks. We can leave with your parents, and complete the house. In the meantime we will have to stay with your family."

Lily was smiling at Bradley. "That is why I love you so. Thank you for being understanding." Her grey eyes hold light brown. "I can deny you nothing Lily."

Margarita was as lovely as ever, she was happy. Lily walks over to her mother, and hugs her. Margarita wonders what brought this on. She stares at her daughter. "So tell me Lily what is troubling you dear?"

Lily looks into her mother's beautiful face. "Nothing I just love you mother." Margarita figures Thomas has told Lily of her illness. Her eyes soften. "Lily you don't have to fret. I will be with you for a very long time."

Lily eyes are misty with tears. "I know that mother. However, we will be moving in a couple of weeks. I want to be there for you." Margarita smiles at her only child. Bradley waits until dinner to tell every one of their plans.

"William we have to leave sooner than planned. We are leaving with Thomas and Margarita. I know this is short notice. Aaron is capable of running the business. We have a couple of weeks left." William and Helen were not expecting this news.

William replies. "Bradley what brought this on? I know that your house is not finished. Is there a problem?" Bradley looks over at Thomas as if he needs support. Thomas intervenes. "William, I asks Bradley and Lily to return sooner than planned, a delicate matter needs their attention.

We can discuss this in private." William offers the library for Thomas and

the rest of the men to discuss the matter.
Thomas explains to William Margarita's
condition. William agrees that this was the
right thing to do. "Let me know if there is
anything I can do to help you Thomas. I'm
at your service."

Thomas holds out his hand to his
friend. William realizes this was a difficult
time for Thomas. Bradley and Lily begin
packing. The two of them were looking
forward to the move. It was time for them to
start their own life together.

Helen talks with Lily and Margarita.
"I shall miss the two of you and my
grandson. I hope that William and I can
come to visit you all soon." Margarita hugs
Helen." You are always welcome to our
home Helen. I would love to see you soon."

Helen offers to help with the
packing, and between the three of them, the
job was complete. Moon speaks with Lily.
"I have a surprise for you." Lily smiles at
her sister-in law. "What is it?" Moon has a
glow about herself.

She was smiling when she tells Lily that she is with child. Lily instantly hugs Moon and congratulates her. "Does Aaron know yet? "Not yet, I'm going to tell him this evening." Lily was happy for them.

Aaron was on his way from the stables with Bradley. He starts the conversation with his brother. "I can't believe the day has arrived for Lily and you to be leaving. I will miss my nephew, and of course the two of you." Bradley has dreamed of this day and he was very enthusiastic.

"I will miss the family also brother, but you and Moon can always visit." "Indeed we will!" Aaron replies. It was dinnertime and this would be the last meal together with Bradley's family. Moon and Aaron make the announcement to the family that she is with child.

The family members perform a toast for Moon and Aaron. Helen was beaming with pride now the house would still have the sound of children in it. Bradley congratulates his brother. "I will be an uncle soon." Aaron was proud that he would be a father.

William and Thomas give Aaron all the advice that a young father should know. The evening passes with laughter and good tidings. Morning was now upon Lily. She looks around the room she and Brad shared. Soon she would be mistress in her own home.

William and the rest of the family were having breakfast when Lily enters the room. Everyone was ready for the journey to Tennessee. Margarita was holding BT. He has become quite fond of his grandmother. After breakfast, the workers load the luggage on the carriage.

After all the goodbyes, Helen and Margarita were both, misty eyed. The women hug each other, and promise to keep in touch. William and Thomas shake hands. Bradley hugs his mother and father. Aaron walks over to wish his brother well. Moon and Lily hug. Moon promises Lily they would come to visit.

Bradley made all the arrangements.
His hands would drive his horses, and cattle.
They board the Train. BT and Lily sit with
Bradley. Thomas and Margarita sit together.
They are ready for the long journey home.
The train slowly pulls into the station.

The group waits for their luggage to
be loaded then ride the stagecoach the rest of
the way home. BT was sleeping quietly
through the ride. When they arrive, Bradley
and Thomas help the women to the house.

Once at home the men unload the
luggage, Thomas notices Margarita looks a
little weary. Lily instructs her mother to rest
for a while, and she would take care of
everything. Margarita thanks her daughter.
Lily put BT down he was sleeping, and she
begins unpacking their clothes.

She was making a list of groceries
for dinner. Bradley enters the room. "What
are you doing love?" "I'm just putting a list
together. I need a few items for dinner."
Bradley takes the list. "How about Thomas
and I go to town, and pick everything up for
you."

Lily

"That would be nice. I will start dinner." "Do you need me to help?" Lily smiles at her husband. "I think I can manage." Bradley and Thomas climb inside the buggy, and start towards town. Bradley notices the shops and the busy pedestrians in the town. It was full of activity.

He decides he could get use to this. Thomas was speaking to his friends, and introducing Bradley. Bradley shakes hands. They were near the market Brad and Thomas pick up the items on the list. The girl behind the counter notices Bradley, so did other eligible women.

The young woman boldly asks Bradley if he was new in town. Bradley raises a quizzical brow at the woman. She was petite slim in stature. She has shoulder length hair, and smooth brown skin. Her eyes are the color of melted chocolate deep dark brown.

Bradley replies. "Yes, my wife and I just moved here." "So you have a wife?" The girl asks. Bradley was amused. "Yes, and this is my father-in- law." Bradley introduces Thomas, although the girl already knows Thomas.

Thomas speaks to the young woman. "Hello, Sandra, I see you have met Lily's husband." The girl gives Bradley that look. Bradley could tell it did not bother her one bit that he was married to Lily. Instead, she sweetly smiles at Bradley. "Well Lily is very lucky. She shouldn't let her husband be out alone."

Thomas is aware the young girl has her sights set on Bradley, so he suggests they should be leaving. Bradley bids the woman good day. Sandra stares after the handsome stranger. She was sure they would meet again.

Meanwhile Thomas and Bradley continue their journey back to the farm. Lily has wonderful smells coming from the house. Bradley brings the rest of the groceries in the kitchen. Then he looks at his wife cooking, as if she did this every day.

"It smells delicious love." Lily replies. "I hope you like it." "I'm sure, I will

love it. I met one of your friends in town."
Lily looks puzzled. "Who might that be?" "I
believe her name is Sandra." Lily wrinkles
her nose. "I would not call Sandra my friend
darling." Bradley decides to leave it at that.

Margarita and Thomas are setting
the table. Margarita pops in to see if they
need her expertise. Lily replies. "Everything
is fine mother. You can help serve if you
like." Bradley hears BT crying, and he goes
to get his son. BT sees Bradley, and he
begins to quiet down. Dinner was delicious.

Lily was a great cook and Bradley
was the first to let her know. Bradley and
Thomas are sitting down for coffee and
brandy. Tomorrow they would start on the
house. The next day as promised Thomas
and Bradley were working on the house.

Bradley was on the roof nailing
while Thomas works on the inside. He hires
a few carpenters to put the final touches on
the house. Lily stops by to see the house.
Bradley climbs down to greet his wife.

Lily replies. "It's beautiful Bradley." Brad was hoping that she would be pleased. "Let me give you a tour of our home love." Bradley holds her hand, and guides her into their home. The rooms were very large and elegant. There was a stone fireplace in each room. The quality of the marble staircase was beautiful.

Lily counts at least six bedrooms. They have a library with cherry bookcases, and full of books. The floors have expensive rugs. The walls adorn with golden framed paintings. The windows are large with leaded glass at the top. The house was fit for a queen.

"Bradley I love it. It is beautiful." Bradley replies. "And so are you love. I am glad you like it. I figure in a week or two we should have it completed."

Lily eyes were bright with happiness finally her world was coming together. "I will be going into town later to pick up more supplies.

Chapter 11

Then I have to leave the rest up to the carpenters. I need to make the transitions for the cattle, and to find buyers. I also have to put together a team to go on cattle drives." Lily knows Bradley was looking forward to the challenge of starting his business here.

Brad was asking Lily. "Would you like to go with me love? You could pick out the material for your curtains, and pick up your dinnerware." Lily was very excited. "Yes darling let me get ready, and then we can go."

Lily put her long hair into a French roll she has spirals of hair down her shoulders. She was wearing a small hat, a long wool suit, and leather shoes. Lily asks her parents to watch BT. Then Bradley and Lily leave for town.

Bradley was talking to Lily. "I have asks your mother to find a nanny for BT. Also we will need a Maid. I think it would be a good idea for us to post an ad in the paper."

Lily agrees. After all, she would have her hands full helping her mother, and taking care of her home. Bradley stops the carriage. He helps Lily down. Together they walk to the shops. They enter a hardware store. Bradley buys supplies for their home, and post fence for his cattle.

The couple was holding hands as they stroll into the fabric shop to purchase curtains. Lily was looking at the fine material silks, and satins. Bradley was speaking with the owner about other accessories. He placed the ad earlier in the paper for the nanny, and Maid.

Sandra Williams was entering the store. She spots Bradley with Lily, and she could not resist the temptation to talk with Bradley again. Sandra immediately saunters over towards Bradley. He was standing next to the owner, in conversation.

Lily

"Hello there, what a small world." Bradley recognizes that flirtatious voice. He turns to see the woman more clearly. Bradley replies. "Good afternoon." Sandra rakes her eyes over his tall frame, and stares into those light brown eyes. She has already decided that she wants him, and determined to have him.

Sandra answers with all the sweetness she could muster. "Bradley, it is so good to see you again. You're shopping alone?" Bradley is astute enough to know this woman wants more than a friendly conversation. "No! Sandra, actually I'm out and about with my wife."

Sandra lowers her lashes, and replies in a surprised voice. "Oh, house shopping? You will be staying then. After all, you are the son-in- law of Thomas. I assume you are staying with them." "Actually we are having a home built." "Really, then we are going to be neighbours."

Bradley could see Lily coming in their direction. Her grey eyes have fire in them. She gracefully walks over to Bradley, and links her arm into his. She was speaking to Sandra. "Hello, Sandra, I see you have met my husband." Sandra was not the least put off by Lily.

The woman boldly confronts Lily, and answers in a derisive tone. "I was just keeping him company while you were away." Lily detects attitude, she replies. "Thank you for being so kind. However rest assured I will not be away for long."

Bradley decides to end the conversation. "Well, Sandra you have a good day. Nice seeing you, shall we go love?" Sandra ignores Lily. "Goodbye Bradley. I'll be seeing you!" The woman watches as the two of them leave.

Lily was angry with Sandra, and the way she openly flirts with Bradley. She goes over the episode in her mind. *How dare that woman disrespect her marriage?* Lily starts to vent her anger. "Bradley, that woman wants you!" Bradley turns to face Lily. His eyes are twinkling with mischief. "Lily love, are you jealous?"

Lily

Lily admits she was very jealous. "I, oh, well, yes I am!" Bradley chuckles with laughter. When he regains control, he replies. "Lily I assure you. Sandra means nothing to me. I am in love with my wife. Let's not ruin a perfect day darling." Lily agrees. Sandra was not going to tarnish her day with her husband.

Bradley and Lily continue touring the city, and all its beautiful sights. Lily notices how the women openly admire Bradley. He was unaware of the women because he was perfectly content with his wife.

Bradley suggests they stop at a steak house to have a bite to eat. He guides Lily through the crowd of patrons. The waiter seats them by the window with a nice view. Lily replies. "I have never eaten here before." Bradley was taking in his surroundings.

A few men approach Bradley. "Good evening sir. Let me introduce myself. My name is Hamilton Myers. I understand you're here from St. Louis, and your father is William Thomas." Bradley eyes are sharp now.

He was paying close attention to the man. "Yes my father is William Thomas. My name is Bradley. Can I help you?" The man asks if Bradley could join them at the City Hall Office later this evening.

Bradley was wondering what this man was after. He thinks on the question before answering. "As you can see Mr Myers, I'm having dinner with my wife. I am very curious as to what matter you have to discuss with me."

Hamilton explains. "It's regarding the cattle business. I think I may be of assistance to you. Your father and I are good friends, and I am in the cattle business."

Bradley shakes the man's hand. "Mr Myers I will be bringing Thomas Kendal along with me." Hamilton has a puzzled look on his face, he knows Thomas Kendal, and if memory serves him right. Thomas was in the crop business.

Lily

"May I ask what does he have to do with this matter?" Bradley was firm. "He is my father-in law! He will be helping with my cattle business." Hamilton admits Bradley was a shrewd man in business. He decides not to press the issue. He replies. "Good day Bradley."

Lily listens to the exchange between the men. "Bradley, are you sure about this meeting." "Do not worry love. I can take care of myself." The couple enjoy their dinner. Bradley orders a Brandy while Lily has a white wine. "Well love, I think we should be heading back. I have to talk with your father when we return."

It was a lovely day with Bradley. The ride home was in silence. Lily and Bradley return to her parent's house. Margarita was holding BT. Thomas was reading the paper. "Hello mother, was BT to much trouble for you?" Margarita replies.

"He is a bundle of joy." Bradley and Thomas need to get down to business. Bradley sits down to go over the meeting he had with Hamilton Myers. Thomas listens to

Bradley and the two men decide they would ride their horses back to town.

Thomas was telling Margarita about the meeting. Bradley walks over to Lily and place a kiss on her lips. "I will see you later love. This is business." "I understand just you two be careful." "I promise." Brad's eyes are warm with emotion.

The two men start for town. They dismount their horses, and enter the City Hall building. Hamilton and the two other men are present. Hamilton offers a hand to Thomas and Bradley. "I'm glad you could make it. Would you like a drink?"

Bradley has a whiskey and so did Thomas. Hamilton introduces the two other men as Claude Williams, and Richard Billings. The men shake hands. Now Bradley cuts to the chase. "Okay, Hamilton what is this proposition that you have?"

Hamilton studies the two men. Then he answers. "I know you will need hands to help with your cattle, and that will require several men. In addition, you will need to find buyers for your cattle. I'm offering you my influence in the community."

Bradley thinks for a minute about Hamilton's proposition. "I have to ask what influence you have." Hamilton replies. "Claude owns the hardware store. Richard is the owner of the paper. I on the other hand own the bank."

Bradley was now seeing clearly. "What is in it for you?" Hamilton takes offence. "Sir I assure you, we are on the up and up here. We are honorable businessmen. Also your father saved my life in the war."

Bradley apologizes for his rudeness. "I would appreciate your help, and Thomas is working on this project with me."

Thomas listens to the conversation. Hamilton agrees. Now Bradley would have the paper at his disposal to advertise for hired help. The bank if he ever needs more finance. It would seem as if everything was falling into place.

Richard Billings joins the conversation. "I will run an ad for you. You will need about twenty men, and a Maid /Nanny. Is that to your satisfaction?

Bradley nods his agreement. Claude Williams offers his services. "I will give you a price cut on your materials. My daughter tells me that you, and Thomas came by earlier."

Bradley's expression closes. He shows no emotion after learning that Sandra was Claude William's daughter. The men end the meeting and every one was satisfied with the arrangements.

After leaving the meeting, Thomas comments. "Bradley, I sure hope you know what you are doing."

Bradley raises one brow at Thomas. "Is there something you want to tell me Thomas?" Thomas thought on the matter before answering.

Lily

"Oh, I have just heard that Hamilton can be cut throat. If you know what I mean." Bradley knows exactly what he means.

"Not to worry Thomas. I have done business with men more cut throat than Hamilton." Thomas believes Bradley was very capable of handling himself. The men ride home, in silence.

Lily was waiting for Bradley to return. "Hello darling did everything go alright?" Bradley smiles at his wife. "It went fine. I think we are on our way love."

Days pass, Bradley was hiring the rest of the men for their cattle drives. The men were putting up new fence, and the carpenters are finished with the house.

Everything was going according to plan. Lily hires the nanny, and the Maid. Bradley and Thomas were supervising the men. Lily and Margarita select the furnishings for the house.

The Furniture arrives to Lily's specifications. The days pass looking after her mother, and family.

BT was getting bigger and more energetic. Bradley invites Thomas and Margarita over for dinner in their new home. Margarita was pleased with the result of their hard work, decorating the house.

The men compliment the women on making the house a grand show place.

Thomas and Bradley are engaged in conversation when there was a knock at the door. The Maid answers the door, and escorts Hamilton, Claude Williams, and Sandra inside. She takes their coats, and guides them to the library.

Another maid informs Bradley of his guests. He walks with Thomas to join the others in the library. Sandra was staring at Bradley when he enters the room. She wears a low cut dress exposing her ample bosoms, and a string of pearls around her neck. Her hair was flowing about the shoulders.

Lily

"Good evening gentlemen. What do I owe this surprise visit?" Hamilton steps forward. "Good evening Bradley, Thomas. We are here to discuss business with the two of you." Sandra takes this opportunity to make her presence known. "Good evening Bradley."

Bradley cocks one brow and acknowledges Sandra. "Good evening Sandra, are you here to visit Lily? She is in the parlour." Sandra knows Bradley is snubbing her, but goes along with it for now.

"Why yes! I would love to see her, and your son." Bradley is aware this was a lie, but he was not concern. Lily could handle herself.

Sandra leaves the men, and Bradley was ready to get down to business. Claude and Hamilton accept the brandy from the Maid. The men turn their attention to the matters at hand. Hamilton starts the conversation.

"I understand you will be going on a cattle drive soon. I am here to see if we can schedule it around the same time. There is safety in numbers."

Brad's eyes never give away his thoughts. "I don't fore see a problem with that. What do you think Thomas?" Thomas looks at the men in the room. "I think that would be alright."

Claude Williams joins the conversation. "Bradley the cattle business is booming right now. I am considering investing in this area. Would you be interested in a partnership?"

Bradley was putting the pieces together in his mind. "I have no need for a partner. I have one hundred fifty head of cattle, and investments in St. Louis that are very profitable." Claude admits that Bradley was no fool.

Hamilton interjects. "You know Bradley a man can never have to many money making opportunities."

Lily

Sandra makes her way to the parlor were Lily and Margarita are sitting. Both women look up at the same time when she enters the room. Lily's grey eyes are sharp, and her face displays a frown.

"Hello Lily, I was in the neighbourhood with my father, and thought I should say hello." Lily holds her composer. "Hello Sandra." Lily introduces Margarita. "This is my mother, would you like some tea?" Sandra graciously accepts the tea.

Lily observes the woman's outfit. She wonders what she was up to now. Sandra directs her comment to Lily. "You and Bradley have a lovely home it is so rich in taste." Lily has known Sandra since they were children.

She was a snob, and never liked Lily. She was always jealous of her looks. The other issue Sandra has with Lily is she is not one whole race.

Sandra was a spoiled little rich girl. Lily replies. "Thank you Sandra, I would show you the rest of our home, but you won't be staying that long." Sandra eyes are daggers. She looks at Lily with distaste, and notes the remark. "Well Lily since my father is doing business with that handsome husband of yours. I should think you and I will be seeing a lot of each other."

Lily's temper was rising. "Sandra you presume too much! My husband's business affairs are just that!" Sandra is aware that she is ruffling Lily's feathers. When she replies her eyes are full of contempt, as she sweetly replies. "Lily I mean no harm, I just thought you and I could become better friends."

Margarita listens to the exchange of words. She decides it was time to intervene. "Sandra how is your family?" Sandra shifts her eyes from Lily to Margarita. "My parents are fine. Thank you for asking."

Sandra pushes Lily even further. "So Lily how did you, and Bradley meet? He is a fine catch." Lily was gritting her teeth when she replies. "It is a long story, and I just don't have the time to tell you Sandra."

The other woman was unperturbed, and she continues. "If I had a man like that I would keep him under lock, and key." Lily was at an explosive level. She has a biting remark on her lips, but the nanny enters the room with BT.

Meanwhile in the library the men conclude their business. Thomas was proud of the way Bradley handles himself.

Hamilton respects Bradley business savvy. Sandra scoots closer to have a look at BT. "He is absolutely beautiful, and he looks just like Bradley." Sandra was sorely testing Lily's nerves. Claude comes to retrieve his daughter. Sandra smiles at Lily as if she has won a battle.

"Goodbye Lily, and Mrs Kendal, very nice to meet you." The woman saunters from the room. Lily breathes a sigh of relief. Bradley was at the door with his guest as the men shake hands, and leave.

Sandra stops to speak with Bradley. "You have a lovely home and your son is adorable." Sandra was looking Bradley up and down flirting shamelessly. Her eyes are full of wanton lust. Bradley replies. "Thank you Sandra, I'm a lucky man."

She sweetly smiles at Bradley, and replies. "You could have a wife, family, and a mistress. Some women don't mind sharing." Bradley was certain this woman was offering herself to him even at mistress status.

His light eyes turn cold. "I have a wife and son! Please do not forget yourself again. Good night Sandra."

She stares at Bradley in disbelief. Was he refusing her? She covers her rejection with an apology. "I'm sorry. I mean no disrespect, Good night." Bradley closes the door, and leans against it for a few seconds. Thomas hears the exchange between Sandra and Bradley.

Bradley was looking at Thomas in disbelief. "I overheard everything. You have

got yourself a problem brewing there."
Bradley throws his hands in the air. "I have
not given that woman any reason to act that
way."

Thomas replies. "I know that
Bradley. She has set her sights on you, and I
don't think it matters to her that you are a
married man." Bradley agrees with Thomas
statement.

They join the women. Lily was just
calming down from the episode with Sandra.
She comments to her husband. "I don't want
Sandra in my home again. She has
disrespected me in front of my mother. She
good as told me, that she wants my husband
at any cost."

Bradley pulls Lily into his arms.
"Well your husband doesn't want her. So the
rest is her problem."

After that, Bradley kisses Lily
passionately on the lips. Thomas and
Margarita could see that all was well with
Bradley and Lily. Thomas announces it was
time for them to be heading home. After her

parents leave, Bradley pulls his wife next to him, and together they walk up the marble staircase to their bedroom.

Bradley was very pleased to be alone with his wife in the privacy of their home. He loosens the pins from Lily's hair, and let her tresses fall down her back. Then slowly he removes her clothing. Lily admits they are overdue for their lovemaking. As Bradley massages her shoulders, and masterfully caresses her body.

Lily's blood was boiling. She tilts her head back to kiss Brads lips. She continues to place light kisses down his throat. While her mouth finds his nipples tantalizing his senses. Bradley draws Lily closer to his body. His strong hands palm her buttocks.

His manhood was erect against her thigh. Lily was moist with desire, and she whispers Bradley's name. He picks her up, and places her on their bed. Bradley opens her legs, and trail kisses from her lips to her lower half.

Chapter 12

Lily was on fire and wanted more, and Bradley gives her everything. His tongue devours her mouth. Lily was at a fevered pitch. Bradley gently enters her warmth, and she was more than ready for him.

Her body reacts to everything Bradley dose. His thrusts are fast, and hard. The sounds of soft moans escalate into loud cries of pleasure from Lily. He takes her to heights she has never known. After he ignites the flames of desire, and she reaches her peak, he joins her.

He was lost in his own passion. Shortly after, he explodes with release. They lay together out of breath, and soon sleep comes. The Next morning, Bradley and Thomas are organizing the men to go on the

cattle drive. Thomas agrees to go with
Bradley on this trip.

He approaches Bradley about joining
him in the cattle business. Thomas has made
a nice fortune now. The men discuss having
a night on the town. They also mention
taking the women to purchase new attire.

After all, they need to dress in
accordance to their status. Bradley admits he
would be doing a lot of entertaining. It was
the part of being a new Businessman in the
community.

The men plan to ask the women to
join them for shopping, and dinner. Bradley
goes home to tell Lily of his plans for the
day. Then he wipes the sweat from his brow.
He needs a bath. Lily was applying the final
touches to the outfit, her hair shines, and she
applies a light lipstick.

Bradley was done with his bath. He
walks into the room with his towel wrapped
around his waist. The water slides off his
lean frame. He was brushing his hair, and
splashes on his cologne. He chooses a

charcoal grey suit, and a white high-collared shirt. He adds gold cufflinks, and his pocket watch.

The only other jewellery was his wedding band. Bradley selects his top hat and his cane with the gold eagle head. Lily and Bradley both admire each other's appearance.

Lily comments on Bradley's attire. "You look very handsome darling!" Bradley in turn replies. "I must say, you look absolutely gorgeous." His eyes have leftover flames of passion burning when he looks at his wife.

He could make love to her right then, but they did not have time. Thomas and Margarita would be joining them shortly. Bradley and Lily walk down the stairs together.

Thomas and Margarita are waiting for them. The couples depart for town. It was a good time for the women to enjoy themselves. Margarita was happy with window-shopping. She stops in a boutique that she has always admired.

Her purchases were small items that she secretly desire. Lily guides her mother to the dressmaker. The men decide on the nearest tailor. The couples agree that the men would meet the woman back at the dressmakers. Bradley lightly brushes his lips against Lily.

"I want you to enjoy yourself, and don't worry about the cost." His light eyes are warm. Lily wonders how she got so lucky, she replies. "I will see you shortly." Thomas and Bradley start for the tailors and other men shops.

Thomas could not believe how well he was doing with the help, and guidance of his son-in-law. The two men talk as the tailor takes measurements for their clothing.

Bradley was use to this life style. Thomas on the other hand was excited. This was a completely new world for him. He was enjoying his newfound wealth. Bradley comments. "Thomas, I do believe we look the part of gentlemen."

Thomas agrees. After the measurements, the men go in the direction of the dressmaker, to meet up with the women. Lily and Margarita were just finishing up with their fittings. The women join the men.

The couples walk to the town's finest steak house. The place was packed. The waiter greets them as they enter the establishment. The owner knows who Bradley is from word of mouth, and he sends a waiter to seat them.

Margarita admires the lovely setting. The room has warm colors, flowers, and people chattering away. Thomas was feeling at ease in his surroundings. Bradley and Lily are happy to see the two of them enjoying their outing. The waiter gives each of them a menu.

Everyone order their favourites Bradley, and Thomas enjoying their steak the meat melts in their mouths. The steak was tender and very juicy. The side dishes are excellent. Margarita and Lily leave the table for the powder room.

The men stand as the women excuse themselves. Sandra enters the establishment. She was with a well-dressed young man. As she walks deeper into the building, she notices Bradley sitting with Thomas.

She was counting her blessing at another chance to get his attention. Sandra was wearing a velvet light blue dress, and her hair up swept in a chignon. Her brown skin was smooth against the material. She was very attractive, with her full lips.

Sandra was still feeling the rebuff from Bradley, and she intends to let him see what he refused. She links her arm in the man's, and make her way over to Bradley.

Bradley's expression goes from friendly to impatient. He notices Sandra approaching his table, and he frowns. Thomas notices the change in mood and follows his line of vision. Thomas spots Sandra and her companion coming in their direction. He instantly knows what caused Bradley's irritation.

Sandra walks over to the men. She replies. "Hello, Thomas." She was looking at Bradley. Thomas returns the greeting.

Sandra continues. "Good evening Bradley, I see the two of you are out for a night on the town." Bradley's expression closes, and his eyes lift to meet the woman head on. As his fingers, gently tap on the wine glass.

Bradley responds. "Yes we are out on the town with our wives!" He makes the statement to deter any innuendos from the woman. Sandra makes an apology for her rudeness. She smoothly introduces the man. "This is Jake Myers, an old family friend."

Sandra was trying to make Bradley jealous. Thomas and Bradley shake the other man's hand, and Sandra sweetly replies. "Where is your wife Bradley? I so want to say hello." Sandra's eyes lock with Bradley. She wants his attention, even if it makes her look the fool.

Bradley raises one brow at Sandra. She was beginning to test his patience. Instead, he smiles showing his even white teeth. "I believe you might get your chance to say hello. She will be back shortly."

Sandra makes an excuse when the waiter approaches. She leaves with a parting shot. "My table is ready maybe another time." Thomas waits for the young woman to leave. "What are you going to do about Sandra?"

Bradley was sipping his wine his brow creased. "I have tried to politely discourage her. It seems I will have to use another method."

Lily and Margarita are returning. Bradley watches his wife coming closer to them. Sandra has nothing on Lily as far as beauty and grace. She was a woman many men admired including him. He would not let Sandra jeopardize his marriage.

When the women settle into their seats, Thomas and Bradley decided not to tell them about Sandra. It was time to start for home. The couples walk out of the steakhouse in good cheer. Sandra was watching as they were leaving.

The more she runs into Bradley the more she desires him. It should be her with a man like that not Lily. Sandra just needs to figure a way to make that happen.

Bradley asks Thomas and Margarita to join them at the house for the night. The two men have a lot of business to discuss. When morning comes, Bradley and Thomas gather the men. It was time to go on the cattle drive.

Lily assures Bradley they would be fine in his absents. Bradley mounts his horse ready to tackle the cattle drive. His mind was sharp. This time would be different for him none of his brothers are present.

Thomas was heading towards Bradley, and his men. The cattle were round up, and the men guide the herds through rough terrain. Hamilton joins Bradley with his herds. The weather has turned cold, and snow begins to fall.

Lily looks through the window as snow softly falls to the ground. BT was resting peacefully. Margarita joins Lily while the men are gone on the cattle drive. The two women give each other strength. They are both praying for their husband's safe return.

Hamilton as promised gives his support to Bradley. This trip would end in Abilene Kansas. The wind and snow whips across the plains, and the snow turns heavier.

They push onward to their destination. Bradley and his men are well armed. They decided to pitch camp. Hamilton was speaking to Bradley and Thomas. "I think we made a wise decision joining forces." Bradley scans the territory. He was wearing his long coat, and ten-gallon hat.

Then he answers Hamilton's comment. "It seems to be a very good ideal indeed." Thomas was helping with their shelter. Bradley joins him. The men secure the cattle for the night. Hamilton starts a fire to stay warm.

Bradley and Thomas decide on rabbit for dinner. The two leave to hunt for their meal. About an hour later, the men return with rabbits in hand. The men skin the rabbits, dress them, and place them over the fire. Hamilton admires Bradley's ability to adjust in any setting.

He was so much like his father William. Hamilton reflects on the war that he and William served in. At one time they were very good friends. Hamilton and William had a parting of the ways, but Hamilton anticipates their paths would shortly cross again.

After all, they would be going through Missouri. Hamilton plans to stop in on William on the way back. Bradley attention now turns to Hamilton. "So Hamilton how many years have you been in the cattle business?"

Hamilton's face has a slight frown. As if he was in thought, then he replies. "For

more years than I care to remember."
Bradley notices the man avoids direct
questions. Bradley continues. "Tell me
Hamilton, why has my father never
mentioned you?"

Hamilton's expression becomes
tense. His wide brown eyes are piercing.
He rubs a hand across his chin before
replying. "We had a difference of opinion,
two young black soldiers with our own ideas
of how to become wealthy men."

Bradley absorbs this information.
He knows the other man was not telling him
the whole story. Hamilton interrupts
Bradley's train of thought. "How is your
mother Helen doing?"

Hamilton expression softens with
the mention of Helen. Bradley notices the
change in attitude with the mention of his
mother. He wonders if William and
Hamilton's disagreement stemmed over
Helen.

Bradley guards his words. "My
mother is well. I plan on stopping through

on the way back. I'm sure William would
also like to see his old friend." Hamilton
digests this information. His expression
remains concealed.

He would finally get to see the
woman he once loved after all these years.
Morning comes, and the men pack up the
provisions. They are back on the trail to
Abilene.

Bradley and Thomas guide the men
and cattle though the harsh terrain. Lily and
her mother rise with the day. It was still
snowing.

Lily wonders how Bradley and her
father are holding up. She knows from the
past that it would be a long time before the
men return. Lily was feeding BT, and
rocking him in the chair. The Maid
announces Lily has visitors.

The uninvited women join
Margarita and Lily in the sitting room. The
nanny takes BT and puts him down for his
nap. The fireplace glows with its warm

ambers. It was Sandra her mother Cynthia, and Richard Billings wife Abigail.

Sandra walks over and extends her hand to Lily as if they were great friends. Her manners are polish.

She introduces the two other women to Lily and Margarita. Lily admits she has to keep herself compose in front of these women. They were Western Tennessee's socialites.

Her mind races, the last thing she wants is to cause her husband any embarrassment. Therefore, she places a smile on her face, and pretends to be pleased with her uninvited guest. After the formalities, the women sit down.

Lily sends the Maid for a fresh pot of tea and pastries. Cynthia and Abigail compliment Lily on her very lavish surroundings.

Sandra starts the conversation. "Lily I'm sorry about not giving you any notice. When I spoke to Bradley the other day, I mention to him that I would be over to say hello. He didn't tell you?"

Sandra has her fine satin dress, and matching hat on. Her eyes hold a gleam of satisfaction. She already knows Lily was in the dark. Bradley never mentioned seeing her at the steak house. Lily's grey eyes conceal her surprise.

She calmly answers Sandra's remark. Lily smiles sweetly, and straightens out her dress before replying. "It must have slipped my mind." Sandra continues. "Well with your husband being a very successful business man. It is your duty to let us introduce you into upper class society.

Lily listens to the other woman. Well, this was it. She wants Lily to join her, and the rest of the rich wives. Lily weighs her words carefully. "It would be an honor to be involved with you ladies. However under the circumstances I feel I would not be much help to you."

Sandra waves her jewel hand in the air. "Nonsense, you would be an asset to us.

Lily, it would just be planning social events and organizing different functions. Of course you and Bradley would mingle with other wealthy business men and their wives."

Lily admits it would help Bradley to entertain his business associates. So she accepts. The women continue their conversations. Sandra was pleased that her plan worked. She was counting on Lily accepting her gracious offer. This would put Bradley within her reach.

After the women leave, Margarita decides, to voice her thoughts on this matter. "Lily dear are you sure you want to be a part of that crowd?" Lily is concern.

"Mother what choice do I have? Bradley will be required to entertain other wealthy men. It will not help him, if I refuse his business partners wives. How would that look?"

Margarita continues. "I don't trust that Sandra dear. Just, be careful Lily. She is after something." Meanwhile Hamilton was quite. The journey was long and dangerous.

Thomas has a few words of his own. "Bradley, what do you think our chances are? Abilene is a very long ways. We have Indians to be concern about, as well as thieves. Need I remind you they are not kind to wealthy cattle ranchers either?"

Bradley has a stern look on his face. He ponders Thomas words before he answers. "God be willing Thomas. I believe that our trip will be a success." Thomas hopes his son-in -law was right. He was beginning to long for Margarita.

He was concern about Lily, and Margarita. Lily was alone to deal with her mother's health problems. He did not want any surprises. Indians approach the men, but they only want to trade furs for some head of cattle.

Bradley was agreeable. Hamilton on the other hand wants to shoot first and ask questions later. His attitude irritates Bradley.

His light eyes turn cold. He was angry at Hamilton's arrogance.

When he speaks, it was through clenched teeth "What the hell is the matter with you Hamilton? You trying to get us all massacred, and for what a few head of cattle?"

Hamilton shifts his gaze at Bradley. The look on his face displays irritation. "I don't agree that it is necessary to give them our cattle for passage." Bradley did not back down from Hamilton.

"Then you fight this battle by yourself. My concern is for all of our safety. I will not have you jeopardize that!"

Hamilton accepts the fact without Bradley he would certainly be out numbered. Hamilton decides this was not the time or place. Weeks pass, the men have completed their journey.

They bought and sold their cattle. Hamilton mentions to Bradley that soon there would be no need for them to go on cattle drives.

The railroad was due to be complete. Ranchers would no longer have to worry about the drives because they could load the cows on the train. The men are heading back now. The weather was still harsh, and so was the terrain.

The men are entering Missouri. Bradley, Thomas, and Hamilton would ride to see his parents. Bradley sends word by his men to inform Lily and Margarita of their plans.

The three men ride long hours until they reach St. Louis. Bradley was approaching his parent's home. The three men enter the house, and Moon greets them.

She hurries over to Bradley, and hugs him. She was glowing with the pregnancy. Moon greets the other men. "Where is Lily and Margarita?"

Bradley explains. They walk deeper into the house together. Aaron sees Bradley, and rushes over to greet his brother. "I was wondering when we were going to see you again. How are Lily, and my nephew?"

Bradley returns the hug, and replies. "They are fine. I just came from a cattle drive in Abilene Kansas. I decided to stop through, and see my family."

Brad introduces Hamilton. Aaron greets Thomas he was shaking hands, and supplies a warm welcome. Aaron has a quizzical expression on his face after meeting Hamilton.

William hears the men talking, and walks in the room to join the group. He observes the four men in his home.

First, he hugs his son, then Thomas. William eyes narrow, and a frown is on his face. William asks. "Hamilton Myers is that you?" Hamilton steps forward. His eyes were full with emotion. "Hello William it has been a very long time." The two men shake hands.

Lily

William invites the men to the
library. Bradley excuses himself. He wants
to see his mother. Bradley finds Helen in the
kitchen instructing the Maids. She turns to
see where the footsteps are coming from.

Chapter 13

Her eyes collide with Bradley's stern ones. Helen's face breaks into a smile seeing her son she was shining with happiness. Bradley steps closer to his mother, and plants a kiss on her forehead. Helen was pleased her son has return.

She asks where Lily and Margarita was. Bradley explains. He takes the opportunity to inform Helen that Hamilton Myers also accompanied him. Helen expression went from joy to apprehension.

It was as if she has seen a ghost. Bradley observes his mother's reaction to the news. Helen tries to regain her composer.

"Did you say Hamilton Myers?" Bradley's light eyes are sharp. He questions his mother reaction. "Mother what is the matter? Who is this man?" Helen was in her own thoughts, so much that she did not hear Bradley's question.

Helen was lost in time, remembering how all this came to be. How could fate be so cruel? She was so young when she met Hamilton. Would her past come back to hurt the people she loves the most?

Bradley repeats the question. "Mother is everything alright?" Helen answers. "Everything is fine son." She walks over to the window, and stares out of it for several seconds before she replies.

"Bradley if there ever comes a time that things are not what they seem. I hope that you can be forgiving. I love you son and sometimes a woman can make mistakes just like men do."

Bradley was at a loss. "What in God's name are you talking about mother?" Helen looks into her son's face, and sees the confusion her words bring to him. She places a hand on his shoulder. "One day soon I will tell you."

Aaron enters the room to collect Bradley and Helen. William was waiting for his wife to meet Hamilton again. Helen smile does not reach her eyes. She acts friendly in front of her family, but inside she is seething with anger.

Helen, Aaron, and Bradley enter the sitting room. She greets Thomas. William puts an arm around Helen's waist, and they both walk over to Hamilton. Helen locks eyes with Hamilton. She was still as beautiful as he remembered.

She silently observes his appearance. There was grey at his temples, but he was still a healthy vigorous man. Helen replies. "Hello Hamilton it is very nice to see you again." Hamilton follows with his pleasantries.

Bradley was standing across the room watching the exchange between his mother and Hamilton. William was also watching his wife's response to the man.

William is aware that Hamilton has a soft spot for Helen.

He looked over Helen, after his injury in the war. William chalks it up as being only that. The Butler shows the men to their rooms.

The meeting ends. The men leave to freshen up for dinner. Hamilton lingers in the room. He wants answers to questions that have been unanswered. The question that has haunted him all these years, was he the father of one of her sons?

Helen was frightful the fear of being exposed gnaws at her. It looks like the past has caught up with her. William and Thomas were having a drink by the fireplace. William was asking Thomas about business in Tennessee. Thomas instantly knows something was troubling the other man.

"William is everything alright with you. You seem to be a little tense." William has a slight frown on his brow. He has no doubts that Thomas was a true friend, and decides to express his worst fears. William begins. "Thomas I have my reservations about Hamilton's motives. I just think it strange that he meets up with my son. Then shows up hear after many years."

Thomas listens to his friend, and thinks on the matter before he responds. "That makes two of us. I question Hamilton's character also, and I do not totally trust him. I try to look after Bradley as best I can." William thanks Thomas for keeping his son safe.

In the meantime, Hamilton was making his way to the parlour. He stands in the doorway watching Helen. She was placing the teacup gently on the table. He accesses every detail, and she was as he remembers delicate, and frail. She was a woman of substance.

Hamilton clears his throat to get her attention. Helen looks up in his direction, and he walks deeper into the room to stand next to her. Helen immediately gets to her feet. Her voice was very low. "Why have you come here?"

Hamilton notes the fear in Helen's face. "I had to come. I had to see you again. I have thought about nothing, but you for over thirty years." Helen's voice becomes hard, and cutting. "I have a husband, home, children, and a good life. Hamilton, please do not jeopardize that."

Hamilton thinks for a minute. "I have no intention of ruining your family Helen. I came here looking for answers about my son. As fate would have it, I met him in Tennessee. Why have you not told him of me? William does not know either, does he Helen?"

Her eyes go wide as he mentions William this news would crush him. The sound of her heart beating fast rings in her ears. This revelation could destroy her whole family.

She begins to panic. "How dare you! How dare you come to my home, and threaten to destroy my family." Hamilton speaks softly to Helen. He could see the conversation was making her upset. "I assure you. I have no intention of threaten you. I' am promising you. If you will not tell Bradley about me then I will."

His large eyes hold fire in them. She is sure he means every word. A few minutes later, she answers in a defeated voice. "Let me be the one to tell Bradley, and William." "Fine, just do it before we leave. He needs to know the truth, and so does William."

Hamilton's anger subsides. He rubs a hand across his brow. "Helen I'm ill and the boy has a fortune waiting for him. Please don't deny him that!" He stares at Helen for a few minutes, and exits the room.

She was alone in her thoughts. There was no way around the truth. It was time to come clean about Bradley's birth. She cups her face in her hands and sobs. Her whole life was one big lie. Bradley joins the rest of his family for dinner. The atmosphere was tense enough to cut with a knife. Helen was unusually quiet, and William was in his own thoughts.

Thomas notices the friction in the air. He excuses himself from dinner early.

Lily

Sensing the family needs time alone. Helen asks Bradley, William, and Hamilton to join her in the parlour. Aaron and Moon look from one to the other something is wrong judging from the undercurrents.

Helen has been acting strange ever since Hamilton showed up. She starts the conversation, and places a hand on Bradley's shoulder. "Son, there are things we need to discuss. I told you there was going to come a time for me to explain things to you. I ask that you to be forgiving. We all make mistakes."

Helen directs her remark to William. She sniffs then starts the conversation. "When William and Hamilton were in the war. William invited Hamilton to stay with us.

I nursed him back to health from his injury. William saved his life. I was a young mother our only child was Aaron at the time. He was a year old when your father enlisted in the war.

Shortly after, I received news that William died in the line of duty. Hamilton was staying with me at the time. I became distraught with the news of William's death, and Hamilton consoled me. We shared one night of passion. I felt so guilty that I ask Hamilton to leave, and the following year the war ended.

William was alive. I was so happy when he returned home safe. I was pregnant with you Bradley. I have lived this lie over thirty years." Her eyes fill with tears, and she chokes out. "Bradley, Hamilton is your father!" She sobs.

William was furious, and in shock. He slumps in his chair devastated by the information. Bradley's light eyes became dangerously cold, absorbing every word. When he finally speaks, it was in a low and calm voice. "William Thomas is my father! He was the one who taught me right from wrong, and how to be a man."

Hamilton tries to calm Bradley down. "I know this is upsetting for you all. Bradley, I do not intend to disrupt your life.

I just want to get to know my son. I am dying Bradley!"

Bradley turns stormy eyes on Hamilton. This was too much to bear and he needs fresh air. After the revelation, a churning feeling was in the pit of his stomach. When he glances over at William what greets him is a devastated man.

Helen was pleading with William. "I never intended to hurt you William. I thought you were dead. I did not mean for this to happen. I was going to take this secret to my grave."

The look on Williams face is deadly. The temptation to slap Hamilton down to the ground where he belongs was there. He inhales a deep breath, and stares at the other man.

Violence was not the answer. Deep down he always had doubts about Bradley's paternity. Over time, he accepts Bradley as his son, and that would not change with this new revelation.

Helen's betrayal would not change the fact that Bradley is his son. William's mind drifts to Bradley, sure, he was hurting from the news, and William would reassure Bradley that nothing was going to stop him from being his son.

Not even Hamilton. William replies. "Even though this is shocking, I let this go a long time ago. My concern is for Bradley. I know he is very confused right now."

Bradley rushes out the room as if the devil himself was after him. His long strides take him to the stables. Aaron notices the look on his brother's face. Something has upset Bradley, and he intends to find out what it was.

Aaron follows Brad to the stables. "Brad what is the matter?" "Not now Aaron! I need a minute to gather my thoughts." Aaron was not daunted. "Brad maybe I can help." Bradley stares at his brother with a tormented look in his eyes.

His brow is creased. "Aaron I was just told that Hamilton is my father. That he is dying, and wants to get to know me better." Aaron lifts one brow after the revelation. His voice is compassionate when he replies. "I know this is shocking news, but it does not change the fact that you are my brother, and William's son."

Bradley thinks on Aaron's words. He was right as usual. Their mother was distraught with the news of Williams's death, and experienced a moment of weakness. Whether he likes it or not the fact remains that Hamilton is his father!

Bradley needs Lily now, and misses her. If she was here, he could face this better. Brad takes a ride for a few hours, using the time to clear his mind.

When he returns to the house, Hamilton and William are in conversation. It seems the two men are dealing with the situation. Thomas and Aaron join the rest of the family.

Bradley walks deeper into the room his expression still shows confusion, but his voice is steel. "I have thought over this matter, and I have no choice, but to accept the situation. However, make no mistake! William will always be my father in every sense of the word." William beams with pride, after all his love for Bradley was as strong as his love for his other sons.

The men discuss many things this night. A week later, Bradley makes peace with his parents. It was time to go back to Tennessee. The three men say their goodbyes and continue the long ride home. Hamilton and Bradley agree to be a part of each other's lives when they returned to Tennessee.

Bradley rides alongside the two men, he was in deep thought. This trip produced a father and half-brother. William was the man he will always consider as his father. Then like turning on a switch, Hamilton enters his life.

Bradley would have to break this news to Lily; he wonders how she will take the news. He thinks of Lily and their son every waking moment. She was always supportive. Thomas realizes Bradley is dealing with a lot right now.

Hamilton rides up closer to Bradley. "Bradley, I will have to break this news to your brother Jake. He has gone through life thinking he was an only child. I just hope he will understand."

Hamilton looks at Bradley with concern. Bradley returns Hamilton stare. His tone was cool and devoid of emotion. "I guess we both have some explaining to do."

The rest of the journey was in silence. Bradley and Thomas finally were coming home. The lanterns burn brightly at his house, he figures Lily is wake, and guides his horse to the stable. He removes his saddle, and rubs the horse down. He places hay in the stall.

Bradley continues his way to the house. Lily was at the door before he opens it. She was beautiful. Her grey eyes are shining with happiness, and love. She smiles at Bradley, and runs into his arms. "I have missed you so darling."

Bradley holds his wife close. He buries his face in her soft long hair, and brushes his lips against hers. The couple walk into the house. Before he closes the door, Lily brings Bradley up to speed. He decides they would discuss Hamilton tomorrow.

Brad mentions to his wife that he was tired, and retires to their room. Lily was happy he was home, and everything could wait. The next morning Lily wakes to BT crying. She hurries out of the bed to check on him, but the crib was empty. *The nanny must have him.* She continues her way down stairs.

She follows her son's voice to the parlour. When she enters the room, she finds Bradley, and their son. He was changing his diaper. He cradles BT, and gives him a bottle. The baby quiets down, and Bradley rocks him in the rocking chair.

Lily sits in a nearby chair and watch Bradley with their son. He immediately looks up, light eyes hold grey. "Good morning love, you sleep well?" Lily is happy to see Bradley taking part in the raising of their son. "I slept fine now that your home." Bradley burps BT, and places a kiss on his forehead then hands him to the nanny.

Bradley asks Lily to sit with him on the sofa. Lily sits next to him on the sofa. He looks directly at his wife, and replies. "Lily there has been some new developments."

She gives her husband her undivided attention. "You are aware that we stopped in on my family—." He pauses as if looking for the right words. "Love, Hamilton Myers is my father, and I have a brother."

Bradley pauses for Lily to digest his statement. "I briefly met Jake at the steakhouse the night we took your parent's to dinner. He was with Sandra Williams. As far as I know, he is unaware of the situation."

Lily's eyes never waver from Bradley's face. She sees the uncertainty in his handsome face; she leaves the chair and kneels down beside Bradley holding his hand. "I'm a little off guard darling. I was not expecting this news. How are you holding up?"

Bradley face is stern. "I'm adjusting, mother explained the situation. She thought William died in the war, and Hamilton was there to console her. She later discovers the mistake in identity. William always knew, but it never changed his love for me. I will always respect and honor William as my father."

Lily lowers her eyes; this was quite a piece of information to comprehend at once. She collects her composer, and places a hand across his brow to smooth out the frown that lingers. She slowly replies. "Are you going to tell Jake that he is your brother?"

Bradley lifts one brow at his wife. His mind has been working overtime since receiving the news. Bradley gets to his feet with Lily beside him. He faces her. "I was thinking we should invite Hamilton and Jake to dinner."

Lily

He waits for his wife's response. Lily thinks on the suggestion. "I think maybe a social evening with business associates, and friends." Bradley was agreeable to the ideal. A couple of days go by, and Bradley takes out time to enjoy with his wife and child.

Bradley did not have to wait for the dinner party to tell Jake, because Hamilton seems to have beaten him to it. Hamilton and Jake are knocking at Bradley's door. The Maid guides the men to the library Bradley was going over some business papers.

He looks up from his work, as the men approach the door. Hamilton walks over to extend a hand to Bradley. Jake was hesitant. Bradley offers his father and brother a seat. He stands to lean against his finely crafted mahogany desk.

He was observing his guest. Hamilton puts his drink down, and clears his throat. "Bradley I have informed Jake that you two are brothers. It would seem that this a good time for the two of you to get to know each other."

Bradley eyes shift to his brother Jake. He was taking a closer look at the man sitting in the chair. What he notices is that they share some features and both have light brown eyes.

Jake was a bit shorter than Bradley was, but just as muscular. Jakes interrupts his thoughts. "Bradley forgive me, I hope you don't think me rude. It has just been a shock to discover I have a brother." Jake admits they share resemblances.

Bradley replies. "I to find this strange, none the less I welcome you as my brother." Jake gets to his feet, and walks over to Bradley. The men hug. "I accept you also." Hamilton was happy that his sons would get to know each other before his death.

Bradley asks the Maid to collect Lily. "I want to introduce you to my wife." Lily enters the room dressed in a blue silk gown with a low bodice. A hair clip holds her long hair. The dress compliments her small waist and wide hips, not to mention her beautiful features.

She is a man's dream. Jake admires the beautiful woman that is his brother's wife. Bradley puts a possessive hand on her waist. He did not miss the appreciation in Jakes eyes.

"Lily, I want you to meet my brother Jake, and my father Hamilton Myers." Lily greets the men with a warm welcome.

"It is very nice to meet the two of you. I hope you will attend our dinner party next week." Hamilton places a kiss on Lily's cheek. "It is my pleasure Lily." Jake walks closer toward the group, he grasp her hand in his then replies. "It is nice to meet you Lily. I would be honored to attend."

Jake looks sincere, after the introductions Lily excuses herself from the men. Jake observes her every movement. She is certainly a very handsome woman.

Chapter 14

Bradley conducts business with his brother and Hamilton. He invites them to stay for dinner. Hamilton makes his apologies, and refuse.

Jake on the other hand accepts the invitation. It was the perfect opportunity to get to know Bradley, and his wife better. Bradley gives Jake a tour of his property. The two men have a lot of catching up to do. Bradley was very observant. He notes his brother's preoccupation with Lily as Jake pulls out her chair.

Bradley decides to let the moment pass, but he would defiantly draw the line when it comes to his wife. Jake was admiring BT. "He is a handsome young man Bradley. I hope you know how lucky you are. You have a woman that loves you, fortune, and a family. You have it all."

Lily

Bradley's face was stern, and he pins Jake with his eyes. The firm smile on his face and the tone of his voice leaves no room for doubt. Bradley loves his family. "Yes, I fully realize that I'm a very fortunate man." Jakes takes the hint. Bradley would protect his wife, and son with his life if need be.

Jake admires this trait. Bradley admits there are a couple of things he likes about his new brother.

Brad discovers there was a couple of year's difference in their ages. Lily is aware that Jake is admiring her. She also notices that Bradley is aware of his brother's advances. The evening goes well. Bradley walks Jake to the door. They say their goodnights.

Lily comments to Bradley. "Jake seems to be nice, so is Hamilton. I think you all will become close in time." Bradley listens to his wife's words. "You are right love. I know it pleases Hamilton that the two of us accept each other. I also know that Jake is infatuated with you."

Her eyes go wide, and she faces Bradley. "Darling you know that you are the only man for me." Bradley hugs Lily. "I know that love! You are a beautiful woman and men can't help it." They walk hand in hand, to their room.

The next morning Thomas was racing to the house, and beating down the door. Bradley hears the pounding and rushes to answer the door. A feeling of dread overtakes him, something was wrong.

Thomas has a look of complete fear on his face. He was standing looking afraid and gasping for breath. Once his breathing settles. He stammers. I, I, need you and Lily to help me with Margarita she is having terrible chest pains.

Bradley guides the man to a chair. He calls for Lily. The three of them go to the house to see about Margarita. Sweat was pouring from Margarita she looks small, and frail. Lily's eyes fill with tears, and she sobs uncontrollably.

Lily

Bradley asks one of his men to send for a Doctor. The Doctor arrives shortly after. Thomas was pacing back and forth, Bradley has no control over this situation and it makes him feel helpless. He comforts Lily and Thomas as best as he could.

The Doctor closes the bedroom door, with a grim look on his face. He looks around at the family then prepares to speak in a quite tone. Lily's heart sinks; instinct tells her this was going to be bad news. Thomas breaks the silence. "Doc what is the matter with Margarita?" Doc's brow creases.

His large eyes are steady on Thomas, and he replies. "I'm sorry Thomas. The best I can do for Margarita is make her as comfortable as possible. She has a bad heart.—." The doctor pauses searching for a way to disclose the other bad news. "Margarita has suffered a stroke along with the heart attack. She is barley holding on. I think it is a good time to call for a priest"…

Thomas almost collapses and his knees buckle. He tries to remain strong as tears slide down his cheeks. Bradley was holding on to Lily her knees turn into water, thank goodness she was in his strong arms. Bradley instructs one of his men to collect the priest. Thomas was at Margarita's bedside pleading for her to hold on. "Margarita, please hang on for me. I need you. I do not want you to leave me.--." He sobs. "I don't want to go without you."

Margarita musters a weak smile her voice is a whisper. "Thomas you have to go on. Do not talk like that. Take care of our daughter and grandson." Thomas holds back the tears in front of his wife. Lily kneels down by her mother's bedside. She could not remember seeing her mother look so helpless, and frail.

Lily touches Margarita's cool hand. "Mother, I love you. What will I do without you? You are my best friend. Who will I confide in?" Her voice breaks into heartfelt sobs.

Tears fall unleashed from her grey eyes. Margarita whispers her last breath. "Lily you have to be strong, and take care of your father for me." Margarita Kendal passes away, and Lily silently weeps. She wipes away the tears, and walks over to her father. She places both arms around him. Bradley takes care of the arrangements for Thomas. He admits this was a difficult time for Thomas, and he was not in any condition to make decisions.

Bradley rides to town to telegram his parent's about Margarita's death. They would be coming to Tennessee for the funeral. Lily asks her father to move in with them, and Thomas agreed.

A week later Bradley's parents arrived, Lily and Bradley were getting ready to pick up his parents from the train station.

Moon and Aaron attend with the rest of the family. Lily was staring aimlessly out the window of her home. She was waiting on Bradley to get ready. It was hard for her to accept that her mother was gone. She would miss her terribly.

Tears softly fall each time she thinks about Margarita, and the reality of never seeing her again. Bradley enters the room. He knows Lily is having a hard time adjusting to her mother's death. He puts both arms around her, and draws her closer against his chest. Bradley gently touches her eyelids with his mouth, and taste the salt from her tears.

"Come, on love we have to go." Lily looks at her husband, and answers in shaky voice. "I'm, I'm ready." They leave for the train station. Helen and William rush over to hug Lily.

Moon tries to comfort her. Aaron gives Bradley a hug, and a handshake. He walks over to give his condolences to Lily. "Lily I'm so sorry for your loss."

Lily thanks the whole family for coming in her time of need. William was speaking to Bradley. "Where is Thomas? How is he holding up?" Bradley replies. "I think he could really use a friend right now father." The family ride in silence to Bradley's home.

Lily

William finds Thomas he looks lost. "Thomas you have my deepest sympathy." Thomas grey eyes are red rimmed and cloudy, but he manages to shake Williams's hand. The men hug. "Thank you all for coming. I know Margarita would have loved to see you."

William admits this was a very difficult time for Thomas. The next day was the funeral, and the family was ready to attend the service. The priest conducts the ceremony. Margarita Marie Kendal placed to rest in their family plot.

Thomas and Lily put flowers on her grave. Helen and Moon cry for the loss of Margarita. Helene and Margarita became close as sisters, and she would miss her friend. Bradley stands by Lily's side. They return to the house. William was asking Thomas to join them when they return to St. Louis.

"You are going to need time away my friend." Thomas admits William was right. "Let me think on it William." William does not push, but would give his friend time to make a decision.

Moon is glowing from her pregnancy. She was there for Lily. Bradley was grateful his family was here.

He was becoming worried about Lily. Moon convinces Lily to lie down, and rest for a while. The family gathers in the living room, and conversation was light. The Maid announces visitors.

Hamilton, Jake, Sandra, and her father Claude come to give their condolences. Sandra rushes over to Thomas supplying sympathies.

Lily was just entering the room from her nap. Sandra performs a grand performance in front of the others. "You poor dear, I'm truly sorry for your loss." Lily did not feel like a confrontation now, she submissively thanks Sandra. Hamilton and Jake join the men.

Bradley introduces Jake to Thomas and his family. Jake was speaking to

Thomas. "I'm sorry for the loss of your wife sir." Thomas thanks the young man. Sandra hides her shock.

The news of Jake being Bradley's brother was the highlight of the evening for her. She converses with Moon and Helen she thinks to herself. *Well this was Bradley's family.* Sandra notes there appearances, judging by the material of their outfits the Thomas clan is well off. Bradley makes the introductions For William, Claude, and then Sandra.

Sandra was speaking to William. "It is a pleasure to meet you. I'm sorry under these circumstances." William acknowledges Sandra statement. Sandra was well aware of the similarities between Bradley and Jake, but Bradley somehow stands out from the crowd.

Bradley continues the introductions, and introduces Jake to Moon. She was absolutely breath taking, but Jake finds his way over to Lily. He was absorbed with her she has his undivided attention. Even in mourning, she was stunning.

"Lily is there anything I can do to help?" Lily looks into Jakes light brown eyes. She thinks. *My goodness he resembles my husband.* "Thank you Jake, but Bradley can supply me with anything I may need."

Helen watches from across the room, and notices Jake's infatuation with Lily. The very thought makes her uncomfortable.

Helen turns her attention to Sandra. It was obvious the woman has eyes on Bradley. She tries to keep his attention as much as possible, hanging on his every word. Bradley's light eyes shift to Lily. He observes his brother Jake trying to hold Lily's attention longer than necessary.

Bradley excuses himself from Sandra's clutches, and manoeuvres toward his wife. Jake's head snaps up staring into Bradley's impatient eyes. Bradley smoothly advises Jake. "I think Sandra is missing you!" Jake was no fool he catches the underlying steel in his brothers tone.

Lily

"Sandra will survive without me. On the other hand I was concern for Lily." Bradley's temper was rising. He would not have his brother pursuing his wife. His jaw tightens, and his gaze was unyielding. "Rest assured Jake. Lily is in very capable hands."

Jake knows not to push Bradley any further. "You are right Bradley; forgive me if I have offended you." Bradley nods his head. The evening passes. The crowd thins out, leaving Bradley, Thomas and his family in attendance.

The days turn into weeks after Margarita's death. Lily puts her hair up in a bun, and dresses warm the days are becoming colder now. Today her goal is to place fresh flowers on her mother's grave.

Lily leaves the house early everyone in the household was a sleep. It was very cold winter was in full swing. Lily slowly walks to the stables, and saddles the mare. Then she mounts her horse, and rides in the direction of the cemetery.

The wind was cold against her skin. She pulls her cloak closer around her. There was a rider approaching as she begins to dismount the horse. Lily kneels to place the flowers on her mother's grave. The thumping of the hoofs is getting louder.

Lily looks up from her task into Jakes face. "Hello, I was on my way to see Bradley. I see you are out and about early this morning." Lily was uncomfortable around Jake, and she stammers. "I, I'm, putting flowers on my mother grave."

Jake dismounts. "I'm sorry Lily. I did not mean to intrude." He moves closer in her direction. The smell of lilac soap assails his nostrils, and a feeling of lust overtakes him.

He wants to hold her in his arms, and touch her sweet lips with his. Lily stands and looks Jake directly in the eyes. "You're not intruding Jake! I have to be getting back. I'm just so lost without mother." Lily begins to cry. She was crying a lot lately. Jake was waiting for any opportunity to get close to Lily, and here it was.

He gently pulls her into his strong arms, and brushes the tears from her wonderful grey eyes. His hand caresses her cheek. Lily was so distraught that she was not aware of what Jake was doing. He brushed a strand of loose hair from Lily's face then lowers his head kissing her fully on the lips.

At first, the kiss was innocent, and then Jake plunges deeper into the sweet nectar of her mouth. Her eyes fly open in shock, and then fear. Jake draws Lily closer intoxicated by the sweetness. His tongue searches her depths, while hands mold her body against him.

Lily starts to resist his advances. Her struggles make him more determined to have her. A hand reaches inside her cloak touching the mounds of her breast. Lily twists free, and soundly slaps his face.

Jake was coming back to reality. His light eyes collide with grey. "Forgive

me Lily." "I should tell Bradley everything."
Lily hissed.

Jake's face turns hard, and
menacing. "I would not do that if I were
you. I can easily persuade him that you
came on to me, and I refused."

Lily's eyes are wide with
indignation. "You would not dare." "I would
dare my sweet Lily. You and I will have an
affair. You can come to me willing, or I will
use force."

Lily was becoming afraid. "What
will you do?" Jake studies Lily features. "I
will simply use all of my influence to make
Bradley believe, that his wife is capable of
infidelity..."

Her grey eyes hold sparks of fire in
them. She was angry. "Bradley would know
that is a lie. I would never be unfaithful to
him." Jake eyes narrow. "Let me put it to
you this way Lily.

Either you summit yourself to me
willing, or I will do everything in my power

to ruin Bradley. Imagine the ridicule of having word spread about an unfaithful wife. I will personal ruin his cattle business, and where will that leave you two?"

She squares her small shoulders facing Jake head on. "Then I will take my chances on telling Bradley the truth about you." Jake digs his fingers into Lily's flesh. His face was set in stone. "You listen to me you little bitch. I am a wealthy man with lots of resources. Do you really want to find out?"

She was scared, and to her chagrin, lost this battle. Lily yanks her arm from Jakes grasp. She was practically at a full run when she mounts her horse. She flees as if the devil was after her. Lily returns to the house out of breath, and heart pounding a mile a minute.

She could not believe what happen to her. Bradley was entering the room. "Oh, love, there you are. I woke, and you were gone. I was up looking for you." Lily gathers her composer. She did not want Bradley to see that she was upset.

She puts a smile on her face before answering Bradley. Lily gives him a kiss on his lips. "I was out putting flowers on mother's grave." "You could have waited, and I would have went with you love." "It's ok darling, I'm here, and everything is fine."

Bradley notices Lily acting strangely. He thought it was from dealing with her loss. The rest of the family was out of bed. Thomas and William went to check on the herds. Helen was holding BT. Moon finds Lily. "Are you alright Lily?" Lily has a frightful look on her face and jumps at Moons question.

"I'm fine Moon thanks for asking." Moon detects something was troubling Lily. She realizes the death of her mother was one, but her attitude has somehow changed. Moon tentatively probes further. "Lily if you need someone to talk to I'm here for you."

Lily wants to tell Moon about Jakes threats and actions earlier this morning. However, she knows it would only cause problems between Jake and Bradley. Instead, she faces Moon, and speaks very softly, "I know you are here for me, and I'm thankful for that."

The women join Helen and Aaron. Helen was speaking with Lily. "Lily, BT is becoming a big boy these days he should be walking any day now." Lily gives a weak reply. Helen notices Lily acting withdrawn, and decides it is time to speak with Bradley on this matter.

Lily was fearful of Jake. Never in her young life has she known this kind of fear. She was at a loss not sure how to tackle the problem with Jake. As soon as Lily lets, Jake drop from her thoughts, he was on their doorstep.

The Maid escorts him to the room. Bradley and Aaron shake hands with Jake, and he plays the role well in front of Bradley. Lily watches under hooded lashes, and seethes with anger. How she dislikes this man.

Jake was greeting the women in the room, but his eyes linger on Lily. Judging from the reception by Bradley Jake was more confident. Lily has not told him of this morning's events. Jake thinks to himself. *In due, time Lily*. He could not wait for the opportunity to present itself again.

As days, past Lily avoids Jake as best she can. Helen was speaking with Bradley. "Son I'm worried about Lily. She has not been herself of late. She seems to be very uncomfortable around Jake." Bradley thinks on his mother's words before he replies.

"I have noticed a change in Lily also. At first, I thought it was the loss of Margarita. Now I'm beginning to wonder." After finishing his conversation with Helen, he decides to address his wife.

Bradley speaks with Lily. "Hello love, take a walk with me." Lily gathers her cloak, and follows Bradley outside. Bradley puts an arm around her shoulder. "Love I know you're having a rough time adjusting to the loss of Margarita. Is there something else bothering you?"

Lily

Lily glances at her husband. How could she tell him? No, she would deal with this herself. Instead, she kisses his lips. "There is nothing wrong sweetheart. I promise." They continue their walk Lily mentions she was getting cold, and they cut their walk short, and head back to the house.

William and his family are departing in the morning. Thomas agrees to join them for a couple of months. The next morning Bradley was taking the family to the train station.

Jake shows up after Bradley leaves, Lily was alone. BT was taking his nap. The Maid shows Jake in. "Hello Lily, you and I need to talk. I am sorry if I over reacted. I want to make it up to you will you join me for a ride."

Lily was about to refuse. Jake senses her hesitation, and he pours on the charm. "I promise to be a complete gentleman." Against her better judgment, Lily accepts his invitation. Maybe they could start over. After all, he was Bradley's brother.

Jake helps Lily on her mare they ride away from the house. He waits for them to be several yards from the house, and grabs the reins of Lily's horse guiding them to an old barn. Lily was furious and replies. "What are you doing Jake?" Jake quickly dismounts his horse, and drags Lily off her mare.

Chapter 15

Lily was struggling with Jake, but he was too strong for her. He was forcing her towards the barn. Lily was kicking and screaming. Jake threatens her to be quite. He places Lily on her feet, drawing her closer to him. Lily was trying to push him away, but his arms are like a steel vice.

"I have long to do this the first time I saw you." Jake begins kissing her neck. His lips roam over hers as his tongue plunges deep inside her mouth. His hands roam over her body, and still she tries to resist. Her body was crumbling under Jakes assault.

Jake loosen the clip holding her hair, it falls about her shoulders, as his hands fumble with the buttons of her dress. Jake expertly pushes away her under things. Lily claws at Jake's face, and screams. He gives an alternative to summit or he would proceed with harming Bradley.

The fight goes out of Lily at the mention of Bradley. She stops fighting him. Her only alternative was to summit. She becomes rigid, from his kisses. Jake runs his fingers through Lily's hair, and lowers her to the soft hay in the barn.

His mouth was on her breast his tongue moves around the nipples suddenly her body betrays her, and a moan escapes her lips. The heat of their bodies was intoxicating. Lily hatred of Jake intensifies.

He was forcing her into an affair that she did not want. He realizes she despise his touch, but still commands her to respond to his lovemaking. He was forcing himself on her, and fear drives her to do what he asks.

Her hands run over the mat of hair on his strong chest. She moves her lips against his throat. Jake removes his trousers. His manhood was firm and warm. Lily was pulling her fingers through Jakes curly hair.

He continues stroking her womanly area. Placing his knee between her legs opening them to receive him, Lily feels the warmth of his manhood against her thighs. Jake was excited beyond his imagination.

Tears slip underneath her lashes as she submits to his assault. Her body continues to respond to Jake. She moves against his manhood.

Jake gently places himself inside moving his hips within, and her hips move back and forth to meet his thrust. Each time he plunges deeper and deeper making her ashamed of the betrayal.

Her body responds to his lovemaking, and he was at his climax moaning aloud, and tugging on her breast. His lips meet hers, as his tongue strokes her mouth into submission.

They reach their climax together. Lily lay next to Jake breathing hard. "This can't happen again. I love my husband." Jake rolls over on one elbow, and look into Lily's eyes.

"I cannot say this won't happen again Lily. I want you more than you know."

"I'm married to your brother, and I love him." "Then why are you making love to me?" Jake puts his finger to Lily's lips. "Don't say anything I want to enjoy you while I can." Jake was ready for round two, and the lovemaking continues.

Jake moans increase as gratification overtakes him with pleasure. He caresses buttocks, and suckles her breast. The position changes as he orders her get on top, and ride his manhood long and hard. Jake pulls her further down on his swollen shaft. Lily gasps with the pleasure of the flesh.

She has to admit Jake satisfied the physical side but she did not love him, and he would never be Bradley. Jake was going to force her to make love to him again, and the thought tears at her heart.

She keeps telling herself, *I am doing this for Bradley.* When it was over guilt, and hatred overwhelm her. She lost the battle of the flesh. Lily detests Jake for his assault on her body.

Shortly after Bradley returns home, but Lily was gone. He searches the house for her, it crosses his mind maybe she was visiting Margarita's grave. Lily was straightening her clothes and tiding up her hair. Jake stands behind her.

He pulls her once again into his embrace, placing his lips on hers in a deep kiss, which promised pleasure. "Lily I want to rip your clothes off, and do it all over again." Lily is aware of the time. She has been gone to long, and needs to get back before Bradley gets home.

"Jake I have to go!" "Meet me tomorrow please. I need you so badly." "I will not." Lily turns her head when Jake tries to kiss her on the lips. He grabs her shoulder once again digging his nails into her flesh. The kiss was hard on the mouth.

"Tomorrow, Lily." "Tomorrow, Jake." Lily mounts her mare. She rides fast to the house. She sees the buggy in front of her home. What was she going to do? Bradley was already home. Lily thinks. *How could I have let this happen?* She loves Bradley! So why was she so attracted to Jake?

Lily was approaching the house. She slides her body from the horse, and slowly walks to the door.

Bradley was waiting patiently for her. "Out for a ride this morning love?" Lily lowers her eyes guilt overwhelms her. Bradley takes in Lily's features, and arches his brow at his wife.

Once again, he patiently waits for a reply. Lily stammers. "Yes, yes, I decided to take a ride yes."

Lily lifts her eyes to stare into Bradley's face. She loves him so much how could she stand in his presence, and lie to him. For the first time since they have been together, Bradley is aware she was not being honest with him.

Lily

Anger was smothering him and he wants answers. "Lily what is going on with you?" Bradley's smooth voice is cutting. His light brown eyes are hard, and his jaw tightens. She knows he is angry with her. Lily walks over to him then she answers in a strained voice. "Bradley, I just can't explain it right now." Lily turns to walk away.

Bradley was infuriated, and moves swiftly, grabbing her arm forcing her to face him. His eyes are cold devoid of emotion, and a frown ceases his brow. "I see you failed to mention that Jake stopped by."

Lily was off guard, and Bradley sees the guilt on her face. His mind was racing as he stares into Lily's eyes. His worst nightmare was eating away at him. Bradley barks at Lily. "You slept with him! You don't have to bother saying anything, I already know."

Bradley pushes Lily away from him; she stumbles forward, and walks out the room without a backwards glance. Lily huddles into a tiny ball. Her heart was breaking. What has she done? Tears fall to the ground. Bradley was hurt tremendously. How could she betray him? He wants to see Jake.

He slams out the front door, and mounts his horse. He rides fast, and hard. Bradley was on his way to Hamilton's house. Once he arrives, he dismounts quickly, walking up to the front door pounding loudly. The butler answers the door, Bradley brush past him.

He goes through the house calling for Hamilton. Hamilton hears the yelling. He meets Bradley in the hallway. "What in God's name is going on?" Hamilton has never seen Bradley in this kind of uproar. "Where is Jake?"

"He is not here right now, come and have a drink. Tell me, what is going on Bradley?" Bradley joins Hamilton, and explains that Jake was having an affair with his wife.

Hamilton was distraught with the information. "Are you sure about this Bradley?" Bradley stares at Hamilton before he answers. "I'm more than sure! I confronted Lily." Jake was arrives and enters the room. His eyes lock with Bradley.

Bradley was on his feet, "You bastard. I welcome you into my life as a brother, and you betray my trust." Bradley did not intimidate Jake. "I love Lily. Yes, I did sleep with your wife, and may I add that she was more than willing." Bradley lost control, and lunges forward striking Jake with force wiping that smirk smile off his face.

His fist meets Jakes chin the two men tussle, and Bradley was getting the upper hand. Jake connects with Bradley face a couple of times, and Hamilton separates the two men. Hamilton was yelling at Jake. "I can't believe you Jake. This is your brother how dare, you pursue his wife."

Jake winded but replies. "I will continue to pursue Lily. I think the choice is hers to make." Bradley is deadly and breaks the silence. "If I catch you anywhere near my wife or son I will kill you Jake." Jake knows Bradley means every word. Bradley turns to apologizes to his father then he leaves his house.

He was on his way to town, in need of a stiff drink. He rides fast and snow swirls in the air from the horse's hooves. Bradley stopped at the local steak house, and orders whiskey. He was drinking heavily trying to relieve his pain. Sandra Williams noticed Bradley at the bar.

The woman makes her way over to him. Sandra inhales a deep breath after noticing the slightly swollen eye. "Hello, stranger what brings you by?" Bradley looks up from his drink to acknowledge the woman standing next to him. "Hello Sandra. What brings you here?" "I see you came in alone. I thought you could use some company."

Sandra was wearing a light pink dress it clings to every curve of her body. The long dark hair flows down her shoulders, and she still wants him. Bradley thought *why not she would do. Why should he refuse her? Lily was not his anymore.* Bradley invites the woman with a smile.

Lily

His light eyes are welcoming. "I would love more than company." Bradley was flirting with the woman aware she wants him. Sandra returns the smile, and licks her lips. "What do you have in mind?" "I was thinking you, and I need to get a room and take it from there."

Sandra was more than agreeable to the idea having Bradley. How long has she waited? It has been months waiting on any opportunity, and finally the moment arrives. Sandra does not know what happen to change Bradley's mind, but glad Lily was not in her way.

Bradley and Sandra agree on the room. Once the arrangements were complete, she agrees to meet in twenty minutes. Bradley orders a bottle of whiskey for later. At the time, the consequence of his actions was the last thing on his mind. All he knew is Lily betrayed him, and it hurt like hell, minutes pass. .

There was a soft knock on Bradley's door, and he answers. Sandra was there as promised. Bradley was not thinking straight, the alcohol dulls his senses. He guides the woman deeper into the room. She stands on tiptoes to kiss Bradley on the lips.

He returns her kisses drawing her against his hard body. Sandra melts against him, being this close heightens her need. A soft moan escapes her lips. "I have waited for this too long." Her tongue was searching his mouth intensifying the effect of the alcohol. He meets the woman's demands.

Sandra was no virgin and clearly experienced in the art of pleasing a man. Her goal is to pleasure Bradley in every sense of the word. Sandra wraps her arms around his neck, drawing him into her.

The warmth of her tongue dips in and out of his mouth while her hands massage his chest, and slides to his lower half. His hands tug against the pins in her hair, and his mouth covers her throat.

She unbuttons his shirt, and feels flesh beneath the palms. Bradley slides Sandra's dress from smooth shoulders, and sends a trail of light kisses along oversized breast. His head lowers to suckle each one. A moan of satisfaction escapes Sandra's lips, as his tongue lightly teases the nipples.

Sandra squirms and moans with the pleasure he was giving. The feel of his strong hands caresses her body stroking her into the flames of desire. He carries her toward the bed once she is settled. He joins her on the bed covering her body with his. Sandra opens her eyes fully to admire Bradley's long lean body. The muscles ripple in his chest as he shifts his hips to explore her curves.

She could not take her eyes off his swollen package. She was in a trace, and her eyes linger on his manhood. There certainly was enough to keep a woman satisfied.

Bradley kissed her lips, neck, and stomach. Once again, he returns to massage her large breast. Sandra could not contain herself any longer. "Please, please Bradley. I need you now." Bradley parts Sandra's legs, and mounts her.

His manhood brushes against her thighs, and she lets out another moan of pleasure. Her body withers, as she moves back and forth. Bradley plunges deep inside her releasing the warmth of his manhood.

She claws at his back. Bradley begins to thrust hard, and fast. His timing is perfect as he moves smoothly against her body.

He could hear his own moans of pleasure and was about to climax out of control. Sandra was holding on to him for dear life. The lovemaking continues, and Sandra never wants him to stop. He was an excellent lover, making her body crave more.

Lily gathers her composer unsure when or if Bradley would return. She hurt him terribly with the deception. Lily rocks their son to sleep. She sends up a prayer that Bradley would listen to her pleas, going along with Jakes blackmail was a terrible mistake.

Lily

Her only hope was maybe she could repair the damage. Lily decides to meet Jake tomorrow. She would not summit to his trickery any longer, and she would tell Bradley the truth.

The next day Sandra crosses paths with Jake. She was on top of the world after sleeping with Bradley, and could not contain herself. The desire to tell someone was tempting, and she just has to share the experience with someone. A warm feeling flows through her when she thinks about the intimacies with Bradley.

Jake greets Sandra "Good morning Sandra you look as lovely as ever." "Hello Jake that is because I shared a night full of passion." Jake eyebrows rise slightly. He hides his surprise, and asks the obvious question with whom? "Okay Sandra I'll bite. Who is the lucky guy?" "Bradley of course, you know how long I have desired his attention. He is absolutely wonderful." Jake light eyes narrow.

"You are kidding me. He's a married man Sandra." Sandra looks her nose down at Jake when she replies. "I think he and Lily are over? Why else would he be in my bed?"

He ponders this information. "It would seem that you are right." "Well of course I am." Jake ends the conversation.

Jake is surprised about the new information. Here Bradley was threating him about Lily, and he was carrying on with Sandra. Jake almost laughs aloud. He would use this piece of information to keep Lily coming to him.

Jake heads for the barn and waits for Lily. She arrives more determined to end this twisted affair.

He stands nearby, and helps her dismount. Lily was beautiful, and her hair swings about the waist. Jake immediately pulls her into his arms. "I was afraid you wouldn't show." Lily notices the bruise on Jakes handsome face. She touches the area. "What happen to you?"

Lily

Jake was face to face with Lily, he notes the concern in her eyes. "Bradley came over the other day. He accused me of having an affair with you. I did not deny it. We fought" "Oh, my God!" Jake was holding Lily tight. I want you right now we can talk later.

She was determined to end this now. "Jake I will not let you bribe me into an affair any longer. I'm telling Bradley the truth!" Jake becomes cold, his eye's glint.

"You will continue as long as I say!" It was time to use his holding card on Lily. "Do you really want a husband that is sleeping with Sandra Williams?"

Lily was horrified. "You're lying!" "No Lily, I am not! I spoke with Sandra this morning. She was ecstatic that Bradley is in her bed." Jake was manipulating Lily again. She begins to tremble.

He takes this opportunity to seduce Lily, and once again, he makes passionate love to her.

She responds to his touch, as he knew she would. Once the lovemaking was over, she admits she has no feelings, or love for Jake, it was fear, and she decides to face it. "I will never see you again Jake! You do whatever you feel you need to do. I am going to see Bradley. I pray he will forgive me. I have been a complete fool."

Jake admits it was over between them. No matter how many times he threatens to ruin Bradley. Lily's love for his brother was too strong to destroy. The look on Lily's face confirms it was over.

He has lost her. Jake concedes. "Lily, let me talk to him. I will tell him the truth. That it was I who seduced you with trickery."

Lily is apprehensive. "You would do that?" "Yes, I would! I cannot ever have you, not completely. Your love for my brother will always stand in the way." Lily leaves Jake. She never looks back. Nothing was worth her marriage or the love she feels for Bradley.

Lily

It has been days since Bradley left Lily and his son. He has taken up residence in Tennessee's finest hotel. Of course, Sandra was a frequent visitor. She leaves Bradley's room just about every night.

Bradley feels nothing for the woman. She was just a stand in for Lily. Even though, she could not ever fill the void in his heart. She was a pale comparison to Lily.

Bradley decides to drop in on Lily and his son. He wears his wide brimmed hat, and matching suit. Once he was satisfied with his attire, he exits his room. Just as he was leaving, Sandra stops by. "Hello sweetheart shall I join you for dinner tonight?" Bradley's light eyes scan the woman's face.

He answers nonchalant. "If you like Sandra, I'm in a hurry." Bradley moves away from Sandra. He was walking down the steps. Sandra stares at him blankly. Bradley admits Sandra thinks they have a relationship. That was the furthest thing from his mind.

He has no love left to give right now. He lost the two most important people in his life. Sandra was indignant Bradley would not treat her like street trash. She runs to catch up with him. He was at the front door. Sandra was calling his name. He stops then turns to face her.

"Darling I know you are not dismissing me? I love you Bradley! Please tell me. You feel the same."

His light brown eyes are sharp, and dangerous. "Sandra, you're a big girl. You are aware that I am a married man." "Yes, but we have become lovers. Don't try and treat me like a common tramp." "I don't have time for this Sandra. We can discuss this matter later. You're making a fool out of yourself."

People are staring at Sandra. She was becoming loud and obnoxious. "I don't care about that! Bradley say that you love me you to." Bradley was losing patience with Sandra. He did not want to make a scene so he indulges her. "Sandra I love you.

Now I have business. Be a good girl, and let me be."

Bradley mounts his horse and rides out of town towards his home. The closer he gets to his house the more he longs for his wife, and son. Lily hurt him badly.

Bradley dismounts his horse. He walks up the cobbled stone walkway leading to the entrance of his home. He opens the door, and enters.

He wants to see his son. Bradley takes BT from the nanny, and sits down, to play with his son. BT was giggling. Bradley hugs him close.

He has no clue what the future holds for all of them. Bradley decides to come to terms with Lily. After all, it was time for decisions regarding their marriage. The Maid went to fetch Lily. Bradley waits for her in the library. Lily enters the room.

Chapter 16

Her hair was on top of her head. Long strands hang loosely about her. She was as beautiful as ever. Bradley takes in her appearance, and begins to yearn for her, his loins ache. Lily sits in the seat Bradley offers her. He was extra handsome today, or was it just that she misses him.

It has been days since they have seen each other, and he seems different. Lily adores her husband; fine time to realize what she feels for him was true love. No one could ever take Bradley's place in her heart.

Bradley was speaking. "Lily, I came to see you, and my son. You know that I will take care of the two of you for as long as necessary." A cold chill runs down her spine. Bradley was talking to her as if he never wants to see her again.

Lily

Fear grips Lily's very soul. Bradley continues. "Under the circumstances, I figure we should come up with an arrangement where I can visit BT. Also, I will be staying at the hotel until you, and I divorce. When the divorce is final, I will be moving back to St. Louis.

Either way I want to see my son." Bradley's light eyes are cold and devoid of emotion. He looks at Lily as if he could not stand the sight of her. She sits quietly, and tears softly fall down her cheeks.

She has lost him forever. She dabs her eyes, and raise long lashes. Grey eyes collide with light brown, "Bradley I know you hate me, and I have hurt you. But please believe me when I tell you, I did this for you." Bradley eyes are hard. He was not in the mood to hear any more lies from Lily.

His voice is harsh, and his handsome face was unrelenting. "Don't, Lily, please have some self-respect. You take me for a fool. I don't want to hear your lies." Lily was horrified, and her eyes are wide. She rushes over to plead with Bradley.

Bradley wants to hold his wife. She was hurting also, but every time he looks at her. He sees his brother making love to his Lily. Bradley stops Lily in her tracks.

"You have heard by now that I'm seeing Sandra Williams. She will be helping me with BT. I know we can be civil about this matter."

Damn! He hates himself for doing this to Lily. Her spirit crumbles under this attack, and her grey eyes are stormy. She places her small hands to her stomach as if he had knocked the wind out of her. Lily gathers all the strength she could muster. She conceals her pain.

When she replies her voice was cool. "Very well Bradley. Will that be all?" Lily wants to end this confrontation as soon as possible. Bradley glances at Lily. *How he loves her.*

His features show none of his thoughts. Bradley continues. "You can have the house. I will gather more of my things. I will be back next week for the rest."

Lily

Lily numbly listens. Then her temper gets the better of her. "You dare flaunt your whore in my face. I hate you Bradley Thomas." Lily admits this was a lie. Bradley studies his wife's reaction.

After her outburst, he is sure she still loves him. Bradley rises. He places his hat on top his head.

"I will show myself out." He leaves Lily standing with her fist clenched. Bradley slowly walks out of his house. His mind filled with pain. He knows that Lily was still very much a part of him, but he just did not want to face that right now. Sandra was waiting patiently for Bradley to return.

He has been gone a very long time. She was hoping Lily was not the reason for his delay. Bradley strolls to his room, after returning from his visit with Lily. He has been in deep thought. He realizes how much he needs her. Sandra is waiting for him, and rushes to greet Bradley.

He was not in the mood for this woman tonight. She could not get enough of him. As Bradley thinks about matter, she was more of a clinging vine. "Darling you're ready of course? You promised me dinner." Sandra bats her eyes, and pouts provocatively.

Bradley enters his room with Sandra right behind him. She was not going to leave, so he takes her to dinner at the steak house. Sandra was in conversation. Bradley pretends to listen to her babbling. Jake and Lily enter the steak house. Bradley catches sight of the other man.

His temper flares. Jake has his hand on Lily small waist. They pass his table Jake was the first to speak. "Good evening Bradley. Hello Sandra." Bradley stares into his brother's face with open hatred he has real nerve. Jake was guiding Lily through the crowd.

Lily smiles up at Jake and her eyes lock with Bradley. Jake was assisting Lily with her chair. Bradley was in a volatile mood now. Sandra becomes angry. She did not like the way Bradley was staring at Lily. He belongs to her now not Lily. "Bradley do you think you can keep your eyes off your soon to be ex-wife?"

Bradley sharply replies to Sandra's remark. "You take too much for granted Sandra! I'm not one of your possessions." Bradley's eyes glint dangerously. Sandra was crossing the line with her comment. She tries to smooth it over. "Darling I only want to love you. I see the pain Lily has caused you."

Bradley was not satisfied with this. He abruptly leaves the table, and walks towards his brother, and Lily. Sandra was at a loss. Jake watches Bradley coming towards their table. Lily could feel the hairs stand up on the back of her neck. She knows Bradley is near.

Bradley glances at Lily, but his eyes are cold. "I see you have found yourself a suitable replacement Lily dear?" Her gaze meets her husbands. What catches her eye is the hurt and pain he was feeling.

She calmly replies to his question.
"Hello Bradley. You have said all you need
to say to me. After all, you don't want me
anymore." Lily voice holds a challenge.
Bradley shifts his gaze to his brother. Jake
was sitting back enjoying Bradley's plight.
"I believe I told you to stay away from my
wife Jake."

Jake returns his brothers stare. "I
think, you, and I agree that it is Lily's
decision. You have no say in it." Bradley
wants to slap that smug look off his
brother's face. Instead, he announces to
Jake.

"Lily is still my wife! You will
permit me to take her to St. Louis." Bradley
quickly reaches out and grabs Lily's hand,
pulling her beside him.

Lily was in shock. Jake interrupts.
"Now hold on Bradley! You can't force Lily
to leave." Bradley moves Lily beside him.
His eyes hold death. "I can, and I will! Lily
get your cloak were are leaving!" Jake stares
at Lily, she replies. "Jake, please don't push

him. I'm leaving with Bradley on my own free will."

Jake was a sore loser, and has no intention to letting Bradley leave with Lily. Jake moves quickly out of his chair. He stands to his full height. "I'm afraid I can't let you take Lily, Bradley."

Bradley was losing patience with Jake. "You have no choice!" Jake pulls a small gun out of his pocket. He aims it at Bradley. Lily sees the cold steel of the gun. Bradley tries to move Lily out of harm's way.

Instead, she moves in front of Bradley and the gun accidentally fires. Lily feels a hot burning sensation all over her body, and pain. All she feels is pain, and her body went limp as she tumbles into Bradley's arms.

The dress Lily is wearing quickly becomes soaked in blood. Bradley continues to hold his wife. Jake was horrified. He never intends to fire the gun. He was trying to scare Bradley with it. Bradley yells. "Get a Doctor!" One of the patrons sends for the Sheriff. The Doctor was on his way.

The Sheriff takes Jake into custody. Jake exclaims. "I never meant to harm Lily, It was an accident." The Doctor arrives. He surveys the crowd, and kneels to check Lily's wounds. She was bleeding badly. He wraps her shoulder, and transports her to the Hospital.

Sandra witnesses the confrontation between the two men. She could not believe what has just happened. Bradley stays by Lily's side, Sandra approaches Bradley, he looks over his shoulder, and sees Sandra his temper flares.

"You can find your way home Sandra Lily needs me." Sandra was upset. How could Bradley be so cruel? He totally forgot about her. All he cares about was his precious Lily. Sandra pulls her skirts, and turns sharply, blinded by tears.

Lily lays motionless. They transport her to the hospital. The Doctor explains to Bradley that they have to hurry. The bullet lodged between her shoulder blades. Bradley runs his long fingers through his wavy hair, and his handsome face looks strained.

He paces back and forth waiting for word on Lily. Hamilton receives the news, and he was distraught. He goes to the jail and demands the release of Jake. After endless paper work, Jake is free on bond. Hamilton and Jake go to the hospital. Jake confesses the whole story to his father.

Jake needs to come clean with Bradley about Lily. He thinks to himself. *My God if she dies. It is my fault.* He pushes these thoughts from his mind. Bradley has been waiting a couple of hours now. Hamilton rushes over to Bradley. "How is Lily? I know what happen between you, and Jake."

Bradley stares into Hamilton's face. "She was trying to protect me."

Jake is the last person Bradley wants to see. He proceeds anyway. "Bradley there is some things you need to know." Bradley was not in the mood for Jake right now. He starts to cut him off. Jake continues.

"Lily was forced to start seeing me. I threaten to ruin you. I made it very difficult for her to refuse me. I just wanted her so badly. I was willing to do anything to have her. She never loved me, and she ended what I forced upon her." Jake takes an unsteady breath and continues.

"She was coming to tell you that I tricked, bribed, and seduced her into an affair. Bradley she only saw me to protect you."

Bradley absorbs his brother's words. Then he scans Jakes face, he was telling the truth. "Why was Lily out with you?" "I came by to check on her. I begged her to continue the affair. She refused. You stopped by earlier, and said the marriage was over. She was upset; I offered to take her out to dinner that is all."

Lily

Hamilton was staring at Jake in disbelief. "Jake I must say you have shamed yourself. I cannot believe you could be so selfish that you would betray your brothers' trust." Jake bows his head. "Father I'm very ashamed of how I acted. Bradley I never meant to harm Lily or you."

Jake extends his hand to his brother. Bradley shakes his brother's hand. Now maybe there could be peace between the two of them.

The Doctor was entering the waiting room. He continues his way towards Bradley. "The bullet has been removed. It does not look as if the bones damaged. She is very lucky.

Lily will have to rest. She has lost a lot of blood." Bradley thanks the Doctor. He asks to see Lily.

The Doctor agrees, but only for a few minutes. Bradley hugs Hamilton then Jake. He continues his way to Lily's room. She lay there peaceful and quite. Bradley walks into the room and sits in the chair next to her bed, covering her hand with his.

Bradley draws her hand to his lips and confesses. "My love, I have been an arrogant stubborn fool. Lily, I need you more than you know."

Her eyes flutter. She was trying to wake up, and faintly hears a voice that sounds like Bradley. Her eyes focus on Bradley's face. She was very weak, but she replies. "Bradley, love you are safe."

His face breaks into a smile showing even white teeth. He waits all night for her to wake. "Hello love, I'm going to have to take care of you. You're not strong enough right now."

Lily musters a smile. "Nothing would make me happier." Then she drifts off into sleep. Bradley leaves the hospital to change his clothes. He is in desperate need of a bath and shave, and rides his horse to the hotel to clean up before going back to see Lily.

Lily

Bradley was just stepping out of the bath, when there was a light tap at his door. He grabs a large towel wraps it around his waist, and answers the door. Sandra was standing there waiting with her hair piled on her head and her hands on her hips.

She wears a dark blue hat and matching suit. Her eyes devour his unclothed body.

She was not about to let Bradley get away she would fight for his affections. The woman saunters into the room. Beads of water slid down Bradley's firm body. "What is it Sandra? As you see I'm in the middle of something."

"I want to see you. Do I need an appointment now?" Bradley was not in the mood for the woman's games. "Is there a point to your coming here Sandra?"

"Bradley, why are you treating me like this? You just told me that you loved me. Do I mean so little to you?" Bradley raises one brow at the woman. She was truly getting on his last nerve.

"Sandra you are a wonderful woman. I am truly sorry if I have hurt you. My heart belongs to Lily, and my son! You can never replace that!" Sandra was reckless now.

"You didn't think about your precious Lily or your son when I was making love to you." Bradley's patience snaps. "Sandra I think you should leave. There will never be anything between you and me."

Sandra looks terrified she did not want to lose Bradley. His lovemaking was the best she had ever experienced. She walks closer toward him pressing her body against his. She cups his face and kisses Bradley passionately on the lips.

Her fingers find his manhood, and enclose around his shaft. She motions back and forth stroking him into passion. Her lustful moans fill his ear. Bradley tries to resist the woman. He was going to push her away from him. Sandra was intent on having Bradley. She moves her hips against his body melting against his muscled thighs. Her tongue slides deep inside his mouth stroking a fire within him. The softness of Sandra's hands glide over the firm manhood like silk. She traces a trail down his stomach. Bradley's blood was boiling.

Overtaken by the sensuality he gasps at the warm wetness of her mouth against his genitals. Her tongue moves up and down circling his large shaft. Bradley feels the warmth as fingers massage his bulging manhood. His body losses the battle of the flesh, and he removes the clothing Sandra was wearing.

Her large breast free from the corset she wore, and his mouth suckles her breast, she moans with pleasure. His breath was warm on her skin.

They end up on the bed. Sandra straddles Bradley. She was moist with desire, and unable to contain herself any longer. Her hips slide over his hot shaft. It fills her very being.

Sandra gasps and moans riding him at a fevered pitch. He feels so good. Bradley was lost in the heat of passion. Each time she leans forward, he would pull Sandra down on his shaft. Each time she would call out his name. Bradley was palming her backside, until he explodes with pleasure. Sandra lay on top of Bradley breathing out of control.

Sandra manages to speak. "Lily can't satisfy you like I can." Bradley got up with a start. My god he has let this woman seduce him. He was not going to leave Lily for her. Bradley rolls off the bed. "Sandra, take your clothes and get the hell out!" She stares at Bradley in disbelief.

"How can you make passionate love to me then disregard me like this?" Bradley was firm his eyes are cold! "Get the hell away from me Sandra! I love my wife, and she is the only woman for me!"

Sandra would not be one of Bradley's playthings. He will not treat her like this. She hisses at Bradley. "You're going to regret you ever met me!" "I already regret it." The woman taunts. "You have no idea how much you are going to regret this Bradley!"

Sandra swiftly puts on her clothes. She leaves the room, and slams the door loudly behind her. Bradley thinks to himself.

What a mess. I must have been crazy to start this with her. He breathes a sigh of relief. At last, he could concentrate on his wife.

Maybe they could rebuild their marriage. Bradley begins to dress then shaves. Sandra walks quickly from the hotel her heart was breaking Bradley has rejected her.

Sandra thinks, how *she hates Lily this was all her fault. Bradley would have learned to love her, if Lily was not in the way.* Bradley finishes up, and stops in for a light meal at the steak house. Jake approaches Bradley "How is Lily doing?" Bradley raises his brow at his brother then he smiles.

"She is recovering." Bradley asks Jake to join him, and he accepts. Bradley pauses as if he was choosing his words carefully.

"I want you to know that, I appreciate everything you said at the hospital, and as my brother I need to be able to trust you. Can I count on your word as my brother, and a man of honor?"

Jake looks Bradley straight in the eye "I give you my word as your brother, and as a man." The two men discuss business Jake asks Bradley about the situation with Sandra.

Bradley replies. "I have let Sandra know there is nothing between the two of us." "How did she take that?" Jake has a surprised look on his face. "I didn't give her any choice."

"Bradley, I have known Sandra a very long time, and she will not let you walk out on her that easy." Bradley raises his brow at his brother then remarks, "Are you speaking from experience?"

Lily

"Regretfully, yes I am." Bradley ponders this aspect. He mentions to Jake that he would be going to his house to check on his son. Jake shakes Bradley's hand, and bids him good-bye. Bradley heads for his home.

When he arrives, Sandra rides up on her stallion. She quickly dismounts her hair was in a loose braid. She is wearing riding pants and tall polished boots. "Bradley, I apologize for my behaviour earlier. I don't want to lose you."

Bradley eyes are guarded. He removes his wide brimmed hat from his head. His wavy hair was neatly in place. "Sandra, I am not interested in your apologies. There was never a relationship. If I misled you in any way I'm truly sorry."

Sandra eyes squint, and her lips tremble. "You are sorry! What is that Bradley? I gave myself to you, and as soon as Lily waves her hand you come crawling back to her."

Bradley's voice was a roar. His face closes, and his jaw tightens. He was at his ropes end. "Sandra, I beg you to please let this go. I feel nothing for you except pity."

Sandra's temper gets the best of her. She raises her hand, and slaps Bradley smartly across the face.

Chapter 17

Bradley yanks Sandra towards him. He holds her hands, and grounds out. "Don't ever do that again Sandra. I might forget that you are a woman."

He releases her, and turns to walk away. Sandra screams at Bradley. "I will tell Lily that I'm with child. What do you think about that?"

Bradley turns around to face this woman. Obviously, she was disturbed. Bradley replies through clenched teeth. "You stay away from Lily! Or I promise you there will be consequence for your actions."

This time Bradley walks away from the woman, and enters his house. He shuts the door behind him, and leans against it. Sandra rides off in a hurry. Bradley has to get the upper hand in this situation with Sandra. She was determined to ruin his life with Lily.

He goes to check on BT, first he feeds his son then reads a bedtime story, and soon he was asleep. He goes to inform one of his men to return to the hotel, and collect his belongings.

He was moving back home. The nanny takes care of BT in his absent. His men are taking care of his cattle. After Bradley was sure, everything was in order. He goes back to town to see his wife.

Lily was softly moaning, the medicine was wearing off, and she was in a great deal of pain. Bradley walks over to her bedside. He places a kiss on her forehead. Lily looks into her husband's smiling face. "What time is it?"

"It's four in the afternoon." Lily has a concerned look on her face. "How is BT?" "He is fine love. I went to check on him. I read him a story, fed him, and he was sleeping when I left." Lily smiles relief washes over her. Bradley pulls the chair closer to the bed.

Lily

"I have moved back home. I think you and I need to get away for a while start over." Her face lights up. "Where do you want to go darling?" "I was thinking of going to St. Louis for the holidays."

"That would be lovely Bradley. Do you think I will recover in time?" "I know you will sweetheart." She becomes misty eyed. "Bradley you know that I love you, and I would never betray your trust." Bradley places a finger to her lips.

"Love, I know why you started seeing Jake. He explained everything. He admits to the whole ordeal. I had no choice, but to forgive him Lily." Bradley runs his fingers through his hair.

"For heaven sakes he is still my brother." Lily looks at Bradley, and her eyes are warm. She waves him closer, and whispers. "That is why I love you Bradley Thomas." "I love you too Lily. I have always loved you." Bradley leans over to his wife, and kisses her lips.

Lily and Bradley talk for hours. It was as if they were rediscovering each other. The day's pass Lily was recovering nicely. Jake and Hamilton stop by to see her, and bring tons of flowers. The Sheriff stops by to see if Lily wants to press charges against Jake.

Lily refuses it was an accident, nothing more nothing less. Today Lily gets to go home from the hospital. Bradley looks as handsome as ever. He walks beside the nurse, and helps his wife into the buggy.

Lily was ready to go home. She misses her son. Things are coming back together for her. She has Bradley back in her life, and her son. She was complete again. Bradley guides the buggy into the front of their home.

He walks over to Lily and carries her inside the house. He climbs the steps two at a time. Bradley gently places Lily on the bed. "I will be helping you into your night clothes." Lily was going to protest. Bradley put his finger to her lips to shush her.

Lily

Bradley carefully takes her clothing off, and put her gown over her head. Then he straightens it out on her. Now he was tucking her under the covers. "You need to rest love. I will be back with something for you to eat. Then I'll bring BT to see you."

Lily lay back on the goose-filled pillows. She was happy to be with her family. A smile touches her lips. "Thank you Bradley" "For what? You would do the same for me." He sits on the bed, brushes his lips across hers, and leaves the room.

Bradley was at an all-time high having his family back. He would never let anything come between them again. He continues his journey to the kitchen, and asks the cook to fix soup, and a light salad for Lily.

"I have to go out for a moment. Look after Lily until I return." Bradley dons a hat, and leaves to check the herds. He makes his way to the stables, and saddles his stallion. He leaves to speak with his hands. Bradley's men are mending a fence when he arrives.

One of his men was telling him that some of the herd had taken sick. They thought it was the fever. Bradley sends for the Vet. He was concerned for his stock. This was his lively hood. Bradley dismounts.

He has a couple minutes with the Vet. The Vet explains that the cattle are only sick from bad feed. Bradley instructs his men to purchase only the top grain. He mounts his horse, and starts heading back to his house. The air was cold and snow begins to fall.

Sandra was riding in his direction. She stops her horse. "Bradley, please don't cut me out of your life. I need you." Bradley could see that this woman never quits. He arched one brow at her.

"Sandra, I will not continue this with you. You are making this more difficult than it has to be." "Well it's difficult for me also. I have fallen deeply in love with you. Can you deny how I make you feel?" "No Sandra I can't deny that.

Lily

There is a difference between lust and love." Bradley I'm with child." Bradley's brows draw together. His eyes are deadly. "How do you know it is mine?" "How could you? You know that we have been lovers for some time." Bradley studies Sandra.

His voice was low. "Sandra it is not like you were a virgin." "So you will abandon your child?" "I will do no such thing. Sandra if you are thinking this will make me leave Lily. You are wrong!" Sandra was clearly upset she was not getting the response from Bradley that she wants.

Sandra pours on the tears, and begins to cry. Bradley tries to sooth the woman. "Sandra what is it you want from me?" Sandra stops the tears as fast as they started. She raises her eye's to meet Bradley.

"I want you to marry me. We are a perfect match." Bradley decided to end this conversation. "I will not leave my wife and son for you Sandra! It is over! If you need money for the child, I will give that to you. That is all."

Sandra replies. "We will see Bradley!" She yanks the reins of her horse and rides like a mad man. Bradley continues his way back to his home. He gives the horses reins to one of his men, and enters the house.

He climbs the stairs to check on Lily. She was still asleep. Bradley decides to freshen up. When he was finish Lily was awake she was eating a little soup. Bradley brings BT to visit his mother. Lily eyes fill with love.

She missed BT the two have never been apart since he was born. Lily hugs her son. After an hour or two, Bradley has the nanny take BT for his bath. It is time to discuss the Sandra situation with his wife.

How would she take the news? If the allegations are true, that he fathered a child with Sandra. Bradley walks over to the window in Lily's room. He stares out of it.

Lily senses something is troubling Bradley "What is the matter love?" Bradley turns to face his wife. His eyes take in the sight of her. How he loved this woman. He did not want to tackle this subject with Lily.

He already knows children are a sensitive subject. Now he must tell her it is a possibility that he fathered a child with Sandra. Lily waits patiently. Her eyes are clear.

Bradley has her full attention. She props herself up on the pillows. Bradley slowly goes over to the bed, and he lies next to Lily. They are facing each other. Bradley places one arm around Lily, and he looks worried.

This was the first time Lily witness her husband drop his guard. "You know how much I love you Lily. We have been through so much together. I would never do anything intentionally to ever hurt you." Lily was afraid. "Bradley, what has upset you so? Whatever it is we can face it together."

Bradley pulls himself together. His voice was steel. I have ended the affair with Sandra. She continually tries to rekindle it.

Her last threat is to tell you she is with child, and it is mine." Lily was appalled.

Her mind goes through a series of emotions before she regains her composer. "Are you sure the child is yours?" "No! I'm not even sure she is telling the truth." "Bradley I didn't come this far to lose you! I love you! We can get through this."

Bradley considers his wife's words then he replies. "Lily I'm preparing you for the worst. I told her I will not leave you, or my son." It was the last straw with Sandra Lily knows what she has to do.

Sandra would not ruin her family. She comforts her husband. The days go by, and then weeks pass. Lily was out of bed now, Bradley was working hard, and BT, was walking.

He was getting his teeth, and was more handsome every day. Bradley and his family would be going to St. Louis in a few days' time.

Lily

Lily gets up early one morning, it was time to pay Sandra a visit, and set record straight. Lily waits for Bradley to go to work. She goes to the stable, and saddles her mare. She was riding to Sandra's house. It was a couple of miles away from them.

Lily approaches the house. She dismounts her horse, and walks up the stairs. Her outfit consist of ridding clothes, and a long coat. The Maid answers the door, and guides Lily to the parlour.

Sandra sits with a smug smile on her face, she was sure that Bradley has come to his senses, and hurries to greet her visitor. Sandra enters the room wearing a chiffon dress with a ribbon on the back it was very lovely.

Sandra thinks to herself. *Bradley is in love with her, and finally realizes she is the right woman for him.* She was sorely disappointed to see Lily waiting for her. Sandra locks eyes with Lily. Inside Sandra trembles, but the look she gives Lily was aloof.

"What brings you by Lily?" "I have a bone to pick with you Sandra." The woman raises one finely arched eyebrow at Lily.

"Is that right? Please, do tell." "I'm here to tell you that Bradley is off limits." Lily's grey eyes are steel. Her chin thrust upward, and her stance is defensive. Lily eye are daggers, and leaves no room for doubt. Sandra observes the woman's features she notes Lily is angry.

Sandra drawls. "And who made that rule?" Lily was losing patience "Let me make this crystal clear. I will fight you every step of the way for my husband. Do you understand me?"

Sandra was blind with rage. "How dare you threaten me? I am soon to be the mother of Bradley's child. He told me he loves me." Lily counters, "If he loves you why then is he with me? You are a pathetic spiteful woman Sandra."

"You say what you will Lily. I will have Bradley. Did he tell you how many times we made love? Did he?" Then Sandra smiles smugly, and continues.

"Did he bother to tell you that we made love while you were in the hospital?" Sandra sees the shock on Lily's face. She smiles triumphantly.

Lily holds her ground. "Obviously, you are not very good at keeping a man Sandra. He ended the affair, face it! Bradley's heart belongs to me, and that is something you can never have."

Lily shatters Sandra's composure. She scathingly looks at the other woman as she sinks down in her chair. She cannot counter the truth. Lily walks out the room without a backwards glance.

She mounts her mare, and starts for home. Bradley greets his wife. "Where have you been love?" "I went to see Sandra." Bradley arches one brow at Lily. He rubs his chin. "Should I ask how that went?"

"It went fine. I think we understand each other now." Bradley knows his wife has a temper. She could be loving and gentle, but she could also be determined. Bradley places his arms around Lily. He lowers his head, and whispers in her ear. "What am I going to do with you?" Lily laughs, and it was a sweet sound.

Together they walk into their house. The preparations are complete for the trip to St. Louis. Lily packs the clothing they would need. Bradley informs her they would be staying for a month at the least. Lily was looking forward to seeing her father, and Bradley's family.

It has been too long. Bradley picks out his grey suit. Lily was wearing a tailored green skirt suit her shoes are finely crafted leather. She puts on her matching hat, and looks breath taking.

Lily dressed BT, and there was a knock on the door. It was Jake and Hamilton Bradley greets his brother, and father. Hamilton replies. "Are you two ready for your trip?" Bradley answers.

Lily

"We are more than ready. You will take care of everything while we are gone?" Jake answers. "Rest assured Bradley. I will personally check on the cattle, and your house."

Jake gives his brother a solid handshake. Hamilton and Jake help with the luggage. They drive Lily and Bradley to the train station. BT was resting quietly. The whistle sounds, and the wheels of the train set in motion. They were heading to St. Louis.

Lily sits next to her husband, and places her hand over his. A smile lingers on her lips. Bradley looks at his wife he was also remembering the first time she came to meet his parents.

Lily opens her eyes to the sound of the whistle blowing. She must have nodded off. Bradley asks if she would like to freshen up for dinner on the train. Lily agrees. She brings the nanny along to help with BT. After she was finished, Bradley was waiting on her. They enter the dining area. It was a grand place. The waiter shows them to their table, and serves wine. Lily was concentrating on the menu.

She was famished. They ordered a lobster dinner, and Bradley takes this opportunity to express his thoughts. "Lily, I want this to be a new beginning for us." "It will be Bradley. I will let the past go if you will."

Bradley looks deep into Lily's eyes. "I already have love." Lily begins feeling light headed. Her stomach was upset, and she feels a little woozy. Bradley notices the strain look on her face. "Are you alright Lily?" "Yes Bradley it will pass. I just feel a little queasy."

"Why don't we go to our room? You need to lie down for a few minutes." Lily quickly agrees. Bradley leads his wife to their room. She exclaims that she is fine.

Bradley insists she rest for a while. Lily quickly recovers. She wants Bradley to love her. "Darling will you join me?" He has waited for Lily to want to make love again. He did not rush her, and was very pleased that she wants him. Bradley feels an instant heat in his loins.

He removes his clothing, and slide between the covers. His strong arms wrap around Lily drawing her closer to his lean body. Lily turns side ways to face her husband. "Bradley I have missed you so." "Lily love you have no idea how much I want to make love to you."

Bradley kisses Lily lovingly on the lips. His strong hands caress her skin. Bradley's kiss deepens. He was igniting a fire deep inside of Lily. She inhales the scent of Bradley soap, and leather mingles with cologne. Lily hands are in his hair.

She loves the feel of his flesh against her palms. He was beautiful, and he was hers. Bradley pulls Lily on top of him, and kneads her breast. His mouth tugs on breast as hands cover her buttocks.

He caresses her soft skin, and his manhood was at full peak. Lily mounts him, and moves with ease. Her long hair brushes his face. Lily gasps, and moans craving Bradley more than ever.

There lovemaking continues into the early hours. Morning comes and Bradley wakes to the sound of the train pulling into the station. He quickly dresses. Lily was with BT. she placed a kiss on Bradley's lips. "Why didn't you wake me?" "You were sleeping so peacefully. I decided to let you rest."

Bradley smiles at his wife. Aaron and Thomas are waiting for Bradley's arrival. The men greet each other. Lily hugs her father. He looks well. Thomas takes his grandson from Lily's arms. "I'm glad you three made it safely."

Aaron gives Lily a big hug. "Moon will be excited to see you. She had the baby. I have a daughter now. We named her Helen Monique Thomas." The trip was starting with good news. Everyone was in the buggy. Aaron drives them to their parent's home. Helen and William greet Lily and Bradley. They continue to the parlour. Moon was there with little Helen.

She was a doll. Moon lets Lily hold her. Bradley congratulates Aaron and Moon. William hugs his son. "Bradley, son I'm glad your family and you could make it for the holidays." Bradley hugs William. "I'm glad to be here also."

William asks the men to join him in the library. There was brandy and cigars. Aaron put his arm on Bradley's shoulder. "I'm glad you will be staying for a while Brad." "You sound as if you have missed me Aaron." "To tell the truth, I have."

The two men laugh, and continue to join the rest of the men. Thomas was shocked to see his grandson was walking, and talking now. His grey eyes twinkle. He thinks of Margarita.

She would have loved to see her grandson. Lily takes BT from her father.

She knows that he wants to join the men. Lily let BT walk over to Helen she was surprised. She quickly grabs him, and place kisses on his chubby cheeks.

William was handing each of the men a drink and a cigar. Thomas refused the cigar, but has a drink instead. Bradley starts the conversation. "Thomas it seems St. Louis agrees with you. You look exceptionally well."

Thomas grey eyes are twinkling. "Yes it has Bradley. William and Helen have been most gracious." William now speaks. "We have been hunting, and fishing. Thomas is a dear friend."

"How is the business going Aaron?" Bradley asks. "I must say it is going quite well. Wouldn't you agree William?" "Indeed, what about yourself Bradley. How is everything in Tennessee?"

Thomas was alert and curious about the business back home. Bradley swirls the glass for a minute. He was not about to disclose all that has happen. He chooses his words carefully. "The business is going well. I have thought about diversifying."

William is a shrewd businessman, and Bradley has his full attention. "What are you thinking of doing Bradley? The cattle business is a good living." "I agree father, however real estate is also a respectable business." William thinks on Bradley words.

He has always made good business decisions. The men end their meeting. Bradley and Aaron walk out together. Aaron was asking Bradley. "You are seriously thinking about getting out of the cattle business."

"I haven't made a final decision yet. I will let you know when I do." Bradley excuses himself, and goes to find Lily, and his son. Lily was sitting with the women when Bradley enters the room.

Everyone gets quite. Bradley stands in the doorway, and arches a brow at the women. A smile tugs at his lips. "Please don't stop on my account." Bradley walks over to Helen, and plants a kiss on her forehead. "Bradley don't worry we will continue in a moment." Helen was teasing her son.

Bradley returns her smile. His attention was on his wife. "Lily, love you up for a walk later." Lily smiles at her husband. "I would love to." Lily decides to freshen up. It has been a long journey. After her bath, she put her hair in a ponytail. Then she wears a long skirt, and matching sweater.

She goes in search of her husband. Bradley meets Lily at the steps. "You ready love?" "Yes, let me get my cloak." Lily and Bradley go out the door. She inhales the crisp fresh air into her lungs.

Bradley noticed how relaxed his wife has become. Lily places her arm around Bradley waist. She enjoys the shelter of his strong arms. "What do you want for Christmas?"

Bradley was asking Lily. "I have everything I need right here with you love." Bradley smiles down at his wife. His eyes twinkle. "Lily you are one of a kind."

"Thank you", she replies. They continue their walk.

Jake was taking care of things for Bradley. He goes to his house to secure everything. Sandra Williams was knocking on the front door. Jake opens the door. "Sandra, what brings you by?" Sandra was surprised that Jake answered the door.

She stares into his light eyes. "Where is Bradley?" "I'm afraid you have missed him. Bradley and Lily are on Holiday." Jake eyes are keen. He knows Sandra is here to start trouble.

The woman was looking at Jake in disbelief. "That can't be! Bradley should be with me." Jake could clearly see Sandra was having trouble with the rejection by his brother.

"Sandra is there something I can do to help?" "Yes Jake there is. You can tell Bradley it was a lie. I am not with child. Jake was utterly surprised. He knew Sandra fought dirty, but he never expected this from her.

Sandra continues. Lily came to see me before they left. She made me realize. Bradley was never in love with me. Tears fall down on her cheeks. Jake knows the feeling. "Sandra I 'am sorry I will tell him."

Sandra gathers her cloak about her, and holds her head high. She leaves without another word. Jake decides to write Bradley with the news. Several days pass. Bradley was opening a letter from Jake.

Bradley automatically thinks there was a problem as he continues reading the letter Jake tells him of the news with Sandra. Bradley breathed a sigh of relief. He goes to find Lily, after he finds her in the parlour.

She has just put their son down for a nap. He walks over to Lily. Bradley was smiling his eyes are carefree. He draws Lily close to him, and hands her the letter to read. Lily was wondering what got Bradley so excited. She scans the letter. A smile breaks on her face. "This is excellent news darling."

Lily

Bradley brushes his lips across hers. "I will never make the same mistake twice. Nothing will ever come between our families again."

Lily looks deep into her husband's eyes. She knows he would keep his word, and so would she. Lily feels relief. She had the upper hand with Sandra.

Bradley suggested they take the buggy to search for a Christmas tree. Lily was agreeable. They ride over the large expanse of land.

Then discover the perfect tree. Bradley takes the axe he brought along, and chops the tree down. Lily helps him load it in the buggy. The couple make their way to his parent's house. Aaron and Thomas help bring the tree in the house.

The women gather to admire the tree, and begin decorating the tree. It was beautiful with the tinsel, handcrafted ornaments gold and silver garland. Presents surround the bottom of the tree, and BT was curious.

Helen replies. "Bradley and Lily you have done an excellent job. It feels like Christmas. Their hearts are full of good tiding, and joy.

Bradley comments, "I wish that Daniel and Thelma could be here." William smiles at the remark then comments. "They will be here tomorrow. I was saving it as a surprise." Aaron and the rest of the family are pleased with the news. Helen face was full of contentment. The family settles into conversation.

The weather was cold and snow falls gradually on the ground. Bradley and Aaron decided they want to pick up a couple more gifts, and they head for town. Bradley desires to give Lily something she would enjoy for years to come.

He selects a diamond necklace, and a formal wedding ring. The stones are exquisite diamonds. Aaron admires the gift Bradley selects, and decides that Moon would look exceptionally nice with jewellery.

Lily

He purchased gold earrings, and a gold wedding ring. The brothers make a couple purchases then head for home. After Bradley and Aaron, arrive. Daniel and Thelma greet them they made it a day early.

Daniel hugs his brothers it has been to long since they all have been together. Bradley notices Daniels appearance. He looks well even gained a few pounds. Bradley asks.

"Where is Emily? How are the two of you doing?" Daniel smiles when he answers. "She is with her parents. Under the circumstances we can't be together here." Bradley could see the sadness in Daniel's face.

He walks over, and hugs his younger brother. Bradley replies. "Then I take it that her parents are still in the dark about the two of you being wed?" Daniel looks dishearten. "Yes they are unaware of our nuptials. I asked Emily not to tell them that way she could always come home.

We have a good life in England. I regret that our families will never know each other. Other than that, I am glad to be home." Bradley could see it was painful for his brother to discuss the situation. Therefore, he changes the subject.

Thelma was gorgeous. She was well dressed, happy, and she has a surprise for her brothers. Thelma links her arm with both of her brothers and walks in the family room. "I have someone I want the two of you to meet."

Bradley and Aaron look at each other. They both are wondering what Thelma was talking about. She walks over to a young man, and guides him towards her brothers. "Aaron and Bradley, I want to introduce you to my husband, Clarence Hastings."

Bradley and Aaron give the man a handshake. They all sit down to be better acquainted with Thelma's new husband. He was and up and coming Doctor. Clarence was proud to be Thelma's husband. He was very polite, and well educated.

Lily

Bradley and the rest of the family welcome Clarence into the family. Christmas morning was welcome in the Thomas household.

The family gathers in the family room to exchange gifts. Today was a blessed event. Lily opens her present from Bradley, and her eyes fill with tears of joy. Bradley helps Lily put on the diamond necklace, and then he formally places the diamond ring on her finger.

He stares deep into his wife's grey eyes. "This is long overdue love. You are the best thing that has ever happen to me." Lily places a kiss on Bradley's handsome face. She holds him close, and replies. "I love you darling, and you are the best part of me." Lily has finally come home.

The End